Roman Holiday

Roman Holiday

Belle Reilly

YellowRoseBooks
a Division of
RENAISSANCE ALLIANCE PUBLISHING, INC.
Austin, Texas

ISBN 0-9674196-3-8

First Printing 2000

9 8 7 6 5 4 3 2 1

Cover design by Mary Draganis

Published by:

Renaissance Alliance Publishing, Inc.
PMB 167, 3421 W. William Cannon Dr. # 131
Austin, Texas 78745

Find us on the World Wide Web at
http://www.rapbooks.com

Printed in the United States of America

To my 'Cheerleader'
and the 'Inscrutable One' –
glad you're in my corner.
I thank you!

Chapter
1

Salvator Mundi was a fine hospital. Clean.
Modern. With state-of-the-art medical equipment, a highly trained staff, and abundant fund-
ing. In Rome, if you were among the best and
brightest, then you were on staff at Mundi. Even
the head dietitian had once worked in the kitchen
of a four-star restaurant in Milano. He'd moved
to Rome and signed with Mundi for the guaran-
tee of better hours and better money. Paid for,
thank you, by the highbrow clientele Mundi
attracted. Socialized medicine be damned. To
the demanding patrician eye, in some quarters
the facility had the looks of a deluxe class hotel,
what with its soft bed linens, large single rooms,

and top-shelf cuisine. Still, it was a hospital, all the same.

And Rebecca Hanson wanted out. Now.

The young flight attendant sat on the side of a hospital bed, her cotton gown discarded, already dressed in a white t-shirt, jeans, and brown leather slip-ons. She was nothing if not optimistic. Becky was surrounded by a small crowd of anxious on-lookers: Mario, the flush-faced local Orbis Airlines representative; Alan Ross, a fellow Orbis flight attendant; a per-plexed, baffled nurse, and one tall, dark, and simmering airline pilot – Catherine Phillips.

"Hanson, I really think you should stay here at *least* another day or two." The pilot's blue eyes glittered, full of frustration at the smaller woman's obstinacy. *What is the matter with her?* Catherine wondered. After all, hadn't it only been a day since she'd taken a hijacker's bullet in the shoulder?

"You should talk," Becky shot back, taking in Kate's bruised appearance... the cut on her brow. The pilot was definitely not putting her best face forward, this day. But Becky had to admit that Kate looked quite... nice out of uni-form, in her putty-colored slacks, lilac blouse, and blazer. "You look like you've been in a prize fight."

Kate snickered. "You should see the other guy."

Becky sighed and shook her head, running a hand through her short, blonde hair. There had been more than one guy, she knew. Four hijackers to be precise, and Captain Phillips had bested them all, saving the lives of everyone aboard Flight 2240 in the process.

"Please, Signorina Rebecca," Mario broke in, a worried look on his face, "Let Orbis take care of you, no? You stay..." he waved his arms around the hospital room, "and soon you be all better."

"I'm all better *now,*" Becky insisted. "That good night's sleep was all I needed." She slipped off the edge of the bed and stood. Kate instantly moved close, to support her if needed, but the gesture was unnecessary. Though still a bit pale, the young flight attendant stood firm. "Let's go," she said.

"No-no-no-no, *signorina.*" The heavy-set nurse moved in, wagging a finger. "You no leave *ospedale* until the *dottore* release you."

"Better listen up, Champ." Alan's voice was dubious. "You don't want to push it."

"Ugh!" Becky tried a different tact. She swept her eyes over the people gathered 'round her, and smiled tightly. "I'm fine. Really. I'm sure getting out of here – taking in some fresh air – will do me a world of good." She shrugged her left shoulder up and down, barely fighting back a grimace. "See? All better."

The effort it took Becky to work her shoulder had not escaped the intense blue gaze of Captain Catherine Phillips. She shook her head. "No way. You get back in that bed and—"

"Please." Becky fiddled with her hospital bracelet, growing more desperate by the minute. "I'm fine. I mean that. I – I just want to get out of here… see a little bit of Rome… put all of this stuff behind me," and her voice broke at that. "Please," she repeated, lifting two beseeching emerald eyes to Kate.

The pilot battled with her emotions. She felt responsible for Hanson, for her safety and well-being. Hell, she owed the younger woman her life. Kate's stomach still fluttered whenever she mentally flipped back to the image of a bloodied Rebecca lying on the floor of the cockpit, unconscious. The wound had seemed terrible then, in those panicked moments before Kate had been able to bring the plane safely down. But Rebecca had been lucky. The bullet had hit the fleshy part of her shoulder and sailed right through. And there *had* been some talk of letting her out today, providing her condition warranted it. Granted, the girl looked much improved over the day before.

"Well…"

Becky arched a hopeful eyebrow at her, and Kate realized that the rest of her audience – including the nurse – also seemed to be awaiting her decision.

Good Lord. "Okay," Kate relented, as Becky heaved a sigh of relief, "IF the doctor says it's all right. We wait for him."

"Fair enough," Becky smiled, folding her arms. "We wait."

This seemed to placate the nurse, who quickly huffed from the room. Mario began pacing back and forth, muttering to himself. His last twenty-four hours had been a public relations nightmare, and these Americans, particularly the dangerous-looking pilot, hadn't made his job any easier.

Alan coughed, nervously, and leaned against the windowsill, gazing out at the bright Italian morning. "So… Bill's gonna be put on a life-flight today, back to the states, I hear," he said, referring to Catherine's first officer who had also been shot by the hijackers. "Probably do him good to be near his family."

"I saw Bill earlier," Becky said, quietly.

"What?" Kate nearly jumped out of her skin. She'd left the young woman alone for barely fifteen minutes, while she'd grabbed a quick shower (thanks to the good graces of a sympathetic nurse) and here Becky had gone off traipsing all over the hospital. "You shouldn't have…"

"He's doing better." Becky's voice was even, her gaze steady. "I needed to see that."

"Oh… yeah." Kate shifted from one foot to the other. "Ah… right."

There was an awkward silence then, punctuated by the occasional page over the hospital intercom. After a minute or so, the nurse returned, with a tall, thin middle-aged man hard on her heels. He wore a tie and a blue dress shirt under a white smock, and his ebony hair was slicked back from a high forehead.

"Dottore Migliani," the nurse stated by way of explanation, ushering him towards Becky. *At this point,* Kate chuckled to herself; *it was hard to tell just who the patient was.* She knew she'd seen better days, and Mario looked as though he were going to stroke out at any moment. It was Hanson who looked the most composed.

"*Buon giorno,*" Becky said, holding out her hand. At first, the taciturn physician looked at the appendage as though it were attached to an alien being. Then, as Rebecca offered him a dazzling smile, his reserve cracked, ever so slightly. A small grin played at his lips as he took her hand.

"Good morning, Miss Hanson," he emphasized the use of his English, and bowed slightly. "If you please…" He waved a hand towards the door.

"Out… out," the nurse clucked. Alan and Mario shuffled towards the door, and reluctantly Catherine started to follow them.

"Stay with me." Becky softly grasped the pilot's arm as she passed by.

Kate stopped.

The doctor raised his eyes in a question mark, but said nothing.

"Sure." She stood at the bottom of the bed while Doctor Migliani poked and prodded Becky, assisted by the nurse responding to his silent cues. Off came the young woman's t-shirt and the doctor nodded approvingly at the healing wound.

"You must keep this dry for the next 24 hours…"

"Okay," Becky said eagerly. Sounded like discharge talk to her.

"… and the stitches will dissolve within seven days. I can give you something for the pain… take one tonight, so you sleep, and thereafter, as needed."

After he applied a fresh bandage, the nurse helped Becky to slip her top back on.

"Does this mean I'm free to go?"

A thin smile passed over the doctor's features. "We were never holding you prisoner, Miss Hanson."

"I – I understand that," Becky laughed, relieved. "You were just doing your job."

"Are there any other special instructions, Doctor?" Kate stepped forward. "Any restrictions on… say… walking or exercise—"

"No," the doctor replied, making notes on Becky's chart. He handed it to the nurse, and nodded. He was through here. "A bit of exercise will do her good." He turned to Rebecca.

"Listen to your body, young lady. When it tells you it's tired, rest."

"I'll listen," Becky said, bobbing her head agreeably.

Kate smiled tightly. "Yes. You will."

"Bene." the doctor grinned slightly. "You are... as you say... free, Miss Hanson." He paused. "Take care of yourself." And with that, he spun out of the room.

As if by magic, an orderly appeared with a wheelchair. "We go now, Miss Rebecca," the nurse said, cheerily.

"Oh, goodness – I don't need that—"

The nurse was about to protest, but Kate cut her off. "Listen, Champ," she said through gritted teeth, her eyes glittering mischievously, "do you want to get out of here, or not?"

"Oooh." Becky glared at Kate, but did as she was told, sinking down into the wheelchair. "My bag—" The orderly was already swinging Becky towards the door, followed by the nurse.

"Mario's got our bags," Kate replied, hustling after them, "Don't you Mario?" She raised her voice as she passed by the chubby Italian lurking outside the door.

"Si, si. Bagagli." He passed a handkerchief across his forehead. "All taken care of, *Capitano."*

"All right, Champ." Alan smiled, pushing his lanky frame away from the doorjamb. "You're outta here?"

"Yep. Eat my dust, Alan." Becky laughed as the little party raced down the hallway, too quickly for Catherine's tastes.

Wasn't Rebecca still a patient? And after all the blonde flight attendant had been through, to risk further injury here, now, thanks to a hot-rod behind the wheelchair, was unacceptable.

"Hey, speed-racer," she grabbed the orderly's wrist, "ease up on the throttle, why don't you?" Whether or not the young, dark-haired Italian spoke English, Kate couldn't be sure. But English wasn't necessary in order for him to understand the iron-grip of her hand, the steeliness in her voice, the darkness in her eyes.

Immediately, he slowed, a glimmer of fear skipping across his face. This was not a woman to be crossed, he knew that much.

"Gosh, Kate, you're no fun," Becky chuckled. She swiveled her head sideways and up, to better take in the tall pilot who strode alongside her.

"You have *no* idea," Kate drolly replied, training her blue eyes straight ahead.

The light-hearted exchange did not escape the notice of Alan Ross. *What's Becky doing, trading jokes with Captain Frosty-the-Snow-Bitch?* Granted, Catherine Phillips had surprised the hell out of him back there, on that plane. They all would have been goners, if it hadn't been for her. She'd shown more guts, been more savvy than the lot of them thrown together.

Well… not including Becky. The Champ had surprised him, too. Then, with her fight and spirit, and now, with her decision to spend some time in Rome, in the company of Captain Phillips. Who would've thought it? And, even more preposterously, the two of them actually seemed to be getting along. What a wonder.

They were nearing the hospital's double-glass entrance doors now, and the entourage slowed. With a *hiss,* the doors opened.

"I bring car around – you wait here." Mario scurried off.

Becky pushed herself out of her wheelchair, fighting off the efforts of the nurse on one side and Kate on the other, trying to help her. "Ahh…" she exclaimed, beaming brightly and breathing in deeply of the fresh, morning air. "It's gonna be a great day."

"After yesterday, I'll say," Alan said, moving closer to her.

The smile faded from Becky's face, and Kate glowered at the young man for bringing up such an unpleasant memory. As if the bandage on Becky's shoulder weren't reminder enough.

Alan caught the pilot's look, and cleared his throat uncomfortably. "Ah… listen, Champ," he shuffled his feet, "I've decided to take the #2260 back to JFK today."

"So soon?" Becky was disappointed.

"Yeah… I was scheduled to work it anyway, so even though I've got the day off now, I thought I'd hitch a ride. I just want to get back home... you know, get back to normal," he finished lamely.

"Joan's going back on that flight too," Kate added, speaking of Joan Wetherill, the hijacked plane's senior flight attendant. "She called this morning to let me know. Same thing. She just wants to get home."

"You need a ride?" Becky asked.

"Nah. I'd rather walk a bit," he sighed heavily. "Anyway... Nathan and Cindy are staying on, for a few days." The two Orbis flight attendants had decided to spend some quality down time in Rome, rekindling a sometimes love affair. And, no doubt, taking the time to recover from their recent ordeal.

"There he is." Kate pointed to where Mario was maneuvering a blue Fiat courtesy car into the circular drive in front of the hospital.

"Well, I guess this is it, then," Becky said, gulping. Impulsively, she threw her arms around the young man, hugging him tightly, tears filling her green eyes. "Th– thanks Alan. For everything."

"For you, Champ," his voice was choked. "Anything."

Mario pulled the car to a stop in front of them; doors began opening and closing as he adjusted bags and seats.

At last, Becky stepped back, ending the moment. "Tell the rest of the gang I said hi."

"You got it." He turned to Catherine, and awkwardly held out his hand. "Thank you, Captain," he swallowed hard, "I'll fly with you, anytime."

"Same here, Ross," she replied, giving his hand a solid shake.

With a final wave goodbye, the young man took off towards the busy street. The nurse moved to leave, too. She handed Kate a small bottle of pills, and a packet of materials and instructions for caring for Rebecca's wound. "You'll be all right from here, Miss Rebecca?" The nurse turned and gestured towards the car.

"I'll be fine, thanks," Becky grinned. "Thanks for everything. *Arrivederci.*"

"Goodbye." The nurse tried in her stilted, accented English, and then she warily swung her gaze up at taller woman. "You be careful with her, yes?" Before Kate could respond, the nurse had spun on her heel and lightly boxed the orderly, bidding him to follow her back into the hospital.

"Ciao." The orderly winked at Becky, quickly skittering away from the pilot's reach.

Becky waved in return, laughing. *"Ciao."*

"Italian men," Kate grumbled, "Don't encourage him."

"Encourage what? He was cute." The blonde turned to the older woman with a smirk, waving an arm out towards the city of Rome.

"And there's a whole lot more where he came from."

"Greaaaat," Kate groaned, but looking down at the sea-green eyes twinkling up at her, she could not prevent a smile from spreading across her face. She blew out a sharp burst of air from between clenched teeth. "Okay," she said, changing the subject, "I thought we'd get ourselves checked into that *pensione* you talked about."

"Oh yeah!" Becky could barely contain her excitement as Catherine gently took her elbow and began guiding her to the Fiat. Mario stood by the passenger door, waiting. "The Ausonia, near the Spanish Steps!"

"That's the one." A light danced in Kate's eyes as she allowed herself to be swept up in the smaller woman's eager anticipation. "I rang them yesterday to tell them you'd been... delayed."

"Thanks," Becky said, pausing as they reached the end of the ramp. Once more, she breathed in deeply of the crisp, morning air, soaking in the sights and sounds of the city bustling so near: the toots of the car horns, the fashionably dressed Italians rushing to work, the sway of the umbrella pines. She was thrilled to be standing on the cusp of a great adventure, delighted beyond all reason at the unexpected company she'd have for it and, very aware of the dull ache in her shoulder with each breath she

drew in, happy to be alive. Never had she held
that sentiment more closely than she did right
now.

"After we get settled in," blue eyes sparkled
down at her, "what do you want to do?"

Becky looked up at the pilot and smiled.
"Everything."

The Pensione Ausonia had been booked by
Rebecca sight-unseen, and when Mario first
pulled up to the tottering five-story building, she
had been more than a little concerned. Creeping
vines clung to the exterior, bits of the aged plas-
ter façade were peeling away and crumbling to
the sidewalk, and the structure itself seemed to
tilt forward into the street, bent like an old
woman. The bright, streaming sunshine shone
unkindly on the *pensione,* highlighting its every
wrinkle and ruin.

Uh-oh, Becky stole a sidelong, worried
glance at Kate. *You wanted native, you've got it,*
she thought, as the pilot helped her out of the
Fiat. If the dark-haired woman had any reserva-
tions about the broken-down building, she didn't
show it.

"That'll be all, Mario, thanks." Kate shooed
the heavyset Italian away from the bags he'd
deposited on the sidewalk.

"Capitano," his wide-open brown eyes
darted back and forth from the pilot to Becky, "if

you need anything... *anything...*" The young man's tie was loosened about his neck and his belly strained at the buttons of his white shirt. Although the sun was not yet high in the sky, he was perspiring heavily.

Kate smiled wanly. "Don't call us. We'll call you."

"*Si...ciao, Capitano...*Signorina Rebecca." He backed away from the two women, dipping his head and waving furiously. He worked his way around to the driver's door, and Becky nearly jumped out of her skin when a small Peugeot came screaming around the corner, narrowly avoiding him. The car beeped angrily at the flustered Italian as it sped by.

"Mario!" Becky cried out.

"S'okay... okay..." Still flashing a dumb smile, he awkwardly maneuvered his bulky form into the car, and drove away.

"I think you put the fear of God into him." Becky nudged Kate in the ribs.

"Hrmph," the pilot mumbled, wagging her dark head. "I'll take credit for the 'fear,' but not the 'God' part." She leaned down and effortlessly hoisted a strapped flight bag onto each of her shoulders, carrying her flight kit and Rebecca's pull-case in her hands.

"Here, let me—" Becky reached for a bag.

"I've got them." Kate smoothly dodged the young blonde's outstretched hand, and struck out towards the door of the *pensione.*

Becky shook her head as she watched the taller woman's broad back retreat into the building. This was going to be a long holiday indeed, if the pilot insisted on constantly babying her.

She followed Catherine into a cool, white-washed lobby, small even by *pensione* standards. Their shoes clicked along the tiled floor as they made their way to a high-topped oaken counter, behind which sat a sixty-ish Italian woman. Her dark hair was streaked with gray, and pulled back into a bun. She wore a straight-lined floral print dress, a blue sweater, and her thin face bore the creases from years of exposure to the sun and cigarettes. She was smoking even now, holding a tapered *sigaretta* in a bony, long-fingered hand. A light cloud of smoke wafted around her, as though she hovered in an other-worldly fog.

"Signora Canova?" Kate let their bags drop to the floor by the desk.

A pair of deep brown eyes stared at her from over a pair of pince-nez chained about the older woman's neck. *"Americanas, eh?"* Clunky gold and amethyst drop-earrings jangled as she spoke.

"Yesss...," Kate paused, before continuing. "I'm Catherine Phillips, and this is Rebecca Hanson. Miss Hanson has a reservation, and I spoke with you yesterday about the delay—"

"Si... si." The proprietress waved her hand dismissively, whirling the cloud of smoke around her. "I remember," she said, in a low,

accented voice. She began turning the pages of a large, leather-bound book that looked to have its origins in centuries past, rather than present.

The *pensione* itself reeked with age, Kate considered, gazing 'round at the high ceilings, the ornately carved mouldings, and the brass-railed staircase that faced the street. A rickety, gated lift stood just to the right of the counter, and to the left side of the lobby was a small dining area. A parlor with a few over-stuffed chairs, sofas, and tea tables lay opposite. Two gray-haired men sat at one table, immobile, silently playing chess.

"I have one room left. *Quinto piano...* fifth floor, number two," she corrected herself in English. The *signora* peered back over her glasses at the two women. "How long you stay?"

Becky looked quickly at Kate before blurting out, "Oh... three or four days, at least."

Catherine lifted an eyebrow at that, but said nothing. Perhaps Hanson was more tired than she was letting on, and needed the additional time to recover. Whatever, Kate had committed to watching over her, and she would not back away from that promise.

Signora Canova put the cigarette in her mouth, and began writing in a light, scrawly hand: 'Miss R. Hanson... Miss C. Phillips...' "You sign here," she said, pushing the book around to face them. Kate took the pen, and then handed it to Becky.

"That will be 100,000 lire per night, no credit cards, payable in full, now," the older woman stated defiantly. "Continental breakfast is served every morning from six until nine."

Before Becky could even make a move, Kate had already laid out the bills on the counter top. "Will this do?"

At last, the proprietress' face broke open in a broad smile. *"Si... si!"* She bobbed her head. *"Benvenuto!* Welcome to the Pensione Ausonia!" She swept the lire back across the counter, and slipped an old, bronze-colored key towards Kate. "Number two," she repeated, making no move to show them to the room. *"L'ascensore,"* she pointed to the lift, *"o le scale"* – the stairs.

"Grazie," Kate said, grabbing the key and hoisting the luggage. She turned for the elevator, and then stopped, realizing Becky was not following her.

"Coming?"

"Ah... I'm okay with the stairs," she said, eyeing the lift dubiously. The pilot had already pressed the button, and ominous clanking and banging sounds were emanating from the shaft.

"You need to conserve your strength," Kate reminded her. "Four flights of stairs can get awfully old, awfully fast." She paused, holding back a grin. "You're not... scared, are you?"

"Of course not," Becky replied, huffily. "I just thought…" And her voice trailed off.

The lift rattled to a stop on the ground floor, and Kate pushed the gate aside. "After you." And she did smile then, allowing the smaller woman to enter the closet-sized lift first. With a bump and a hiss, the lift was off.

"Great," Becky said. "If this is the elevator, I can't wait to get a load of the plumbing."

"Are you sure there *is* plumbing?" Kate was intently examining a small spot on the ceiling of the lift, carefully avoiding Becky's glare.

The young blonde blushed deeply at the pilot's words. It had been good enough when she thought she'd be alone to get a room in a small *pensione,* versus a large hotel. The thought of going native, of being absorbed into the local culture, had appealed to her then. But even she had been taken aback by the Ausonia's tired appearance, and she was embarrassed for the sake of the tall, elegant woman standing next to her. Surely, Captain Catherine Phillips was used to the best things in life, whether they be clothes, cars, or companionship. The elevator labored higher and higher, but Rebecca Hanson's heart sank with the humiliation of knowing that she'd dragged the pilot slumming with her. Oh God, how would she ever get over this. She ought to suggest that they leave right now, go someplace else.

With a sighing groan, the elevator clanked to a stop. "We're here," Kate said, cheerily. She had noticed Becky's increasing discomfiture in reaction to the ambiance of the *pensione.* Quite frankly, she was enjoying it. While there was no doubt that she welcomed the amenities of a first class hotel, she'd also seen her share of the underbelly of what military housing had to offer, thanks to her early days in the Air Force. Compared to some of the places she'd seen, the Ausonia, so far, was a damned castle.

The women stepped from the lift into a carpeted hallway, blanketed in light streaming in from a floor-to-ceiling Palladian window at the end of the corridor.

"Hmmm..." Kate said, appreciatively. "Nice." She walked slowly along the hall, examining the room numbers, while Becky glumly followed behind. "Looks like this is us," she said, stopping in front of the last door near the window. She slipped the key into an old brass lock.

Rebecca could stand her misery no more. "You know, Kate, why don't we just leave here and— omigod!" Her hand flew to her mouth in shock.

"I know," the pilot stepped into the room and dropped their bags to the floor, "awful, isn't it?" She turned to Becky and grinned. "You were saying?" She pulled Becky in and shut the door behind her. "Not quite the Hilton, eh?"

The room was stunning.

A snapshot of classic, old-world Italy, their room was all cream-colored walls, and antique oak and ash furniture, balanced with a delicate needlepoint rug in the center of the floor. A gilded mirror dominated one wall, while double glass doors opposite led out onto a small balcony.

The ceiling had to be at least nine feet high; *a benefit of being on the uppermost floor, no doubt,* Kate thought. On it, a central fresco of ancient Rome was framed by the rest of the ornately carved ceiling and moulding, overflowing with a riot of grape leaves, vines, and sunbursts.

A small sitting area was tucked in a corner, near a low-silled window that reached upwards to the crown moulding. The window was cracked open, and a gentle breeze parted lace curtains, allowing golden sunlight to warm an oak writing desk and a pair of easy chairs. A drinks table in front of a beige divan held a bottle of San Pelligrino, several glasses, and a bowl filled with grapes, apples, walnuts and crackers.

Kate and Becky mutely wandered to one door – a walk-in closet. Another led to the bathroom. It was there the women received a second shock.

"This is as big as my apartment's living room," Becky gasped. The young woman stepped onto polished terra cotta floor tiles and gazed around the bath. The porcelain fixtures were of classic design: a claw-footed tub with shower attachment, a pull-chain commode, a pedestal basin, a heated towel rack and, of course, the requisite bidet. A wicker basket holding a variety of soaps and bath salts sat on a marble shelf jutting out from the wall. Next to the basket was a stack of fluffy white towels and washcloths.

Catherine walked back into the room, shaking her head. "100,000 lire, right? About $55 dollars. You heard it too?"

"Yeah, can you believe it?" Becky squealed, pushing past her and lifting the latch on the balcony doors. "Oh gosh," she sighed, flinging them open wide. "Unbelievable."

Kate followed Becky out onto the deck, beautifully framed in by a wrought iron, scroll-work balustrade. A pair of all-weather chairs was arranged around a small table, which was decorated with a potted plant. Becky leaned on the railing, taking in the view below. She let the breeze ruffle her hair, the sun warm her skin.

"What is it?"

"The Piazza di Spagna," Kate said, easing her arms down on the rail next to Becky. "Look there." She casually put her hand on the younger woman's back, and pointed. "The Spanish Steps."

"Beautiful," Becky breathed, and indeed, it was an impressive sight. The *piazza* was closed off to motor traffic, but the cobbled square was teaming with people in the late-morning sun. Students, professionals, tourists, children – even the occasional dog – formed a sea of humanity, flowing and ebbing on the midday tide.

In the center of the square was a large fountain featuring a half-sunken boat that was noisily spouting water. The steps themselves were dotted with groups of young people reading, drawing, chatting. Photographers, espresso drinkers, friends and lovers, gathered here at the traditional meeting place as had their forebears for the past two centuries. Twelve flights mounted upwards towards a renaissance-style church on the *piazza* above; budding azaleas were just beginning to bloom along the length of the steps as they journeyed there.

Kate still held her hand lightly on Rebecca's back; for some reason she hadn't been inclined to move it away. She felt the young woman begin to tremble.

"What is it?" she asked, alarmed. "If you're chilled—"

"No," Becky said, turning to look up at her with moist, green eyes that looked like gemstones in the sunlight. "I… I just can't believe I'm here. That… that we made it…" She started to cry in earnest.

Kate hesitated for only a moment. Yes, Hanson was a weeper, but God knew she had good reason to be, after what she'd just been through. "Sssh… there… take it easy now," she whispered as she reached out to the smaller woman.

The pilot was surprised at how quickly Becky responded; at how comfortable the girl felt in her arms as she embraced her. After all, Catherine Phillips was not normally the touchy-feely type. "C'mon now… don't cry." She stroked the short blonde hair. "It's okay… you made it. Everybody… made it."

After a time, Becky's sobs quieted, and at last the girl pulled slightly away. She let her arms drop to Kate's waist. "Thanks," she said, forcing a smile to her tear-streaked face. "I know I'm just… being silly, I guess."

"No you're not." Kate gave Becky's arm a squeeze and stepped away. "You've been through a lot the past couple of days. It's only right that you should be a little…" she groped for the right word, "emotional."

Becky laughed aloud at that. "Emotional. That's me."

"Listen, why don't we freshen up, and then go out and see some of the sights? Maybe grab a little lunch?"

"Sounds good," Becky said, moving back through the doorway, wiping at her face. "I was hoping you couldn't hear my stomach growling."

"Oh, that's what that was." Kate latched the doors closed behind them. "I thought it was some heavy construction equipment out on the *piazza.*"

"Ha," Becky said, flouncing down into an overstuffed chair. She reached for a bunch of grapes from the bowl, kicked off her shoes and propped her feet up on the table's edge. "You ain't heard nothin' yet." She plunked a grape into her mouth. "I snore."

"Now wait a minute," Kate growled in mock anger, shrugging off her blazer. "That was not in the brochure I saw." She sat down on a chair next to Rebecca and poured two glasses of mineral water.

"Sorry," Becky said simply, taking the proffered beverage. "Must've been the beta version."

"You rat," Kate laughed, pitching a grape at the young flight attendant. Becky nimbly caught it, and made short work of it. "Still," Kate eyed the sweeping floral canopy that hung over an ornately carved four-poster bed – the only bed – in their guest-room, "maybe you would be more comfortable if I slept here." The pilot gestured towards the divan.

"What?" Becky was stupefied. "Don't be silly. You'd have to be a contortionist to fit there. There's plenty of room in the bed."

"But your shoulder... what if—"

"Nonsense. You're not killing yourself over here. Either we're both in the bed, or both out of it," she insisted, gazing firmly at Kate's blue eyes. "Now, what do you say?"

Kate briefly contemplated the image of an injured Rebecca Hanson bunking on the floor of the room, well carpeted though it was, and she cringed. "The bed it is," she sighed, closing her eyes. "You don't play fair."

"I play to win," Becky chuckled. "Remember, this is the Champ you're talking to." And with that, she pushed herself out of the plush chair, and headed towards the bath. She lightly brushed Kate's shoulder as she slipped by. "I won't be a minute, and then we can hit the streets. Sound like a plan?"

"A plan it is," Kate groaned, smiling under her still-lidded eyes. As she listened to the receding patter of Becky's feet, the pilot thought it curious that she could still sense where Becky's fingers had made contact with her shoulder. The girl had such a sweet, innocent way about her, and already Kate could feel how she was chipping away at the stony exterior of her reserve, an image she'd worked so hard to cultivate. With each passing moment, Catherine was feeling more and more like the façade of the Ausonia. Crumbling under the gentle spirit of Rebecca Hanson. *Dammit.* She couldn't afford to let her guard down. Not now. Rebecca Hanson didn't deserve to have any more pain in her life. She would watch out for her, see her through this, and that was it.

Hurt. That's what happened to people who got close to Catherine Phillips. Hadn't she seen the results of that time and time again? Finally, she'd stopped trying at all. She couldn't stand the pain she seemed to bring to people's lives. Her family. Friends. Come to think of it, she didn't much like the feeling herself.

Better to avoid it entirely.

That's the ticket, Kate thought, reaching for another grape. *Keep on running.*

Chapter
2

Rome wasn't built in a day, and they sure as hell weren't going to see it in a day, Kate knew that much. Regardless of Becky's ambitious touring designs, the pilot had every intention of keeping the pace slow and undemanding, for Hanson's sake. The younger woman had obviously planned for some intense sightseeing; she'd produced a backpack from her luggage and filled it with a small 35mm camera, tour books, maps, bottled water, and a light jacket.

"Sunscreen?" Kate had turned up her nose when she saw Becky stowing it in her pack. "Never use the stuff."

"No kidding," Becky blithely replied, taking in the tall woman's bronze skin. "I'll bet you've never been burned in your life."

"Well, not by the sun, anyway," Kate chuckled. "Here, give me that." And before Becky could protest, Kate snapped up the filled backpack. She was wearing her long, dark hair loose, and she swept it out of the way as she shouldered the bag. "Can't have you hurting yourself."

Becky opened her mouth as if to speak, then thought better of it. Kate was probably right. She was still feeling a little achy, and she'd be darned if she'd let the pilot know it. There was too much she wanted to do this day.

Becky convinced her companion that taking the stairs down would not be too taxing, and so they clattered down the marbled four flights with ease. When they hit the lobby, Rebecca headed right for the front door. After a moment's consideration, Kate decided to interrupt Signora Canova's latest cigarette.

As she approached the large, oaken desk, she could see the older woman peering at her from above her pince-nez. She was smoking, yes, the billowing cloud around her was proof enough of that, but she also had been reading a newspaper. Quickly, she folded it and put it aside.

Kate coughed. "Ah… thanks for the room," she said, eyeing the gray-haired woman closely. "It's lovely."

"All of the Ausonia's rooms are *bello,*" she said indignantly, pushing a stray wisp of hair back into her bun. Her dark brown eyes darted from Kate to the newspaper and back again, and Kate turned to it too.

Splattered on the front page, was a screaming Italian headline about the hijacking. There was a photo of the gaping hole in the fuselage of the Orbis 777-200 jet and, next to it, an old head-shot of Kate. God, it must've been taken when she first joined Orbis. Below the pilot's picture, the face of Rebecca Hanson smiled out at her.

Ugh. Publicity. the tall woman thought, pretending she hadn't seen it. Obviously, Signora Canova had. Perhaps that accounted for the upgrade in their room.

"Look," Kate changed the subject, "is there a place nearby where we could get something to eat before sightseeing?"

"*Si,*" the *signora* replied, still a bit testy. She waggled a spindly finger towards the door. "Down past the steps, go left, and right... you will see the *tavernetta.* Food is good, yes?"

"*Grazie.*" Kate adjusted the pack on her shoulder, popped on a pair of aviator-frame sunglasses, and headed outside to catch up with Rebecca. The young woman smiled up at her. "Let's go."

Kate took Becky to the restaurant by way of the Spanish Steps, and the flight attendant insisted that Kate pose for a photo at the bottom.

"I'm going to ruin your pictures of the sights if you keep that up," the pilot grumbled, but something told Becky that was far from the truth.

The *piazza* was lined with food and wine shops, boutiques, and restaurants. "Ooh... I can't wait to go shopping," Becky said, eyeing them greedily, "but I need some sustenance first."

A few stops and turns later, there was the *tavernetta* Signora Canova recommended. Kate led the way, selecting pasta in a walnut and cheese sauce. She paid the attendant, got a slip, and then moved to the end of a counter for her dish. Becky followed along, pointing to a pasta and eggplant concoction for her entrée. In short order, the two women had redeemed their slips for lunch, and were relaxing at a table near the street with some fresh bread and mineral water.

"Oh God, this is fantastic," Becky said, twirling her pasta and munching away.

"Not bad," Kate smiled into Becky's green eyes, teasing her. The food was delicious. From the moment they'd walked into the place, her mouth had watered at the cooking smells: the oils, the roasted peppers, and the breads.

"Well, what you don't want, I can finish for you," the younger woman replied. A pause and then, "So... you've obviously been to Rome before."

"Yeah," Kate turned her eyes away at that, "a few times."

"For work… or pleasure?"

"Work. Definitely work." Kate realized that the younger woman expected her to elaborate. She took a sip of water, and bent to lift the backpack off the floor, placing it on an empty chair. A constant stream of Italian working people was making its way in and out of the small restaurant, brushing closely by. "I used to be in the Air Force, stationed in the north, at Aviano."

"The air base that's been in the news recently." Becky's voice was solemn, referencing the Balkan conflict.

"Mm-hmm. Anyway… I was able to pick up the language a bit… get down to Rome a few times," Kate finished, leaving it at that.

Rebecca could sense that there was a deeper story there, but by the way her companion's eyes had clouded over, she decided to leave it alone for the time being. She reached into the backpack, and retrieved a large notepad. "Well," she twirled another bite of her pasta, "it's painfully apparent that I've never been. So, what I thought we could do…" and she began to read off a laundry list of activities.

"Whoa, there." Kate grabbed the notebook from her and held it up for examination. "Is this for the rest of the week?"

"No," Becky replied, blinking her eyes. "This afternoon."

The pilot snapped the notebook shut and replaced it in the backpack. "No way."

"B – but…"

"No buts. You've been through a lot the past couple of days, and I don't want you wearing yourself out."

"Kate," Becky was whining now, and she hated herself for it, "I'm fine. The Forum, the Colosseum—"

"Will still be there tomorrow." The tone in Kate's voice told Becky that the older woman would brook no argument.

Silently, Becky pushed her plate away, deeply disappointed. So much for Rome. So much for the things she'd wanted to do. And so much for thinking this Captain Frosty could ever be her friend. She turned to gaze out at the street. At the people. Anywhere, to avoid having to look into the eyes of Catherine Phillips.

"Look… I'm sorry." A lower tone now, apologetic, and Becky could feel a warm hand slip over her own on the table. She tried not to respond to it but, somehow, just the simple touch of the pilot's palm drew her back in.

She lifted her eyes to the dark woman. "Forget about it."

"No…" Kate pressed. "I – I guess sometimes I have to think about how something's gonna sound before I say it. I'm not used to just… talking." A pause. "What I meant to say is… that we can still sightsee today. We can do some shopping, go to some of the places in this area of the city… but not stray too far from home base. I'd rather wait on the more vigorous stuff... until tomorrow, even."

"That sounds fine." Becky found her resistance melting away under the woman's earnest admission.

"Hell, Hanson," Kate continued hoarsely, "you just got out of the hospital this morning. I want to see you all better – not any worse." Now it was Kate's turn to blink and look away.

Rebecca felt about two inches tall. How selfish of her, pushing, pressing to meet her own agenda, not realizing the effect it might be having on the captain. After all, she hadn't had the easiest flight of it either, Becky realized, eyeing the fading bruise and thin scab on the pilot's forehead. It hadn't occurred to her that her companion might not exactly be feeling up to par either, though Becky decided to keep that thought to herself. No use in mentioning it at all, for Kate would surely deny it.

"Hey," Becky said, turning the tables on Kate and clasping the larger hand in her own. "I have an idea." She gave the hand a squeeze.

Kate swiveled her head back to the younger woman. "Well?"

"Your plan for today sounds great. The last thing I want is to overdo it, and not be able to enjoy the rest of our time here. So how about today, the *piazza,* and tomorrow, the world." Her green eyes sparkled.

Catherine could not help but smile at her companion's enthusiasm. And finally, the girl was seeing the sense in taking it easy for the day. That took a load off of Kate's mind. "Deal," she replied, a silly grin over-spreading her face. "What are we waiting for?"

The women walked back along the Via de Macelli towards the Spanish Steps area, where they revisited many of the shops and boutiques they'd passed by on their way to lunch. They took their time nosing about in several art and antique galleries, before Kate finally put her foot down. "Clothes," she said. "One of us did not pack enough for this little holiday."

Becky was only too willing to allow herself to be steered down the Via Condotti towards the Via del Corso. She loved to clothes-shop, but after a bit of walking, even she was over-whelmed by the heady concentration of the fashion elite and their emporiums.

"Oh wow," Becky exclaimed, as they strolled by plate-glass window displays chock-full of the latest styles and fabrics, "how do you know what to wear?"

"Oh, don't worry," Kate rumbled. "They'll tell you."

All the top designers were represented: Versace, Ferre, Laura Biagiotti, with prices that – lire or no – took Becky's breath away. The young woman swallowed hard. "Look, if you want to stop in any of these…."

The tall woman laughed. "Around the corner here," she pointed to the del Corso, "there are some nice shops that aren't quite as pricey. They'll do fine."

"Oh, good," Becky gulped in relief. "You know," her shopping mode kicked in once again, "I could use another outfit for nighttime…"

Merona was the first shop Kate led them to, a smaller boutique with a mix of mid-range designer wear and *prêt-à-porter*. The exotic-looking sales associates spoke English – a necessity in this cosmopolitan part of the city – and two women instantly descended upon Kate and Rebecca, only too willing to direct them towards a variety of fashionable ensembles.

Half an hour later, Kate was ready to blow her top. "I'm just looking for a few outfits for touring!" she said for the tenth time, as a tall, bone-thin saleswoman – several inches taller than the pilot – flashed her a sleek, full-length evening dress.

"But dear," the clerk crooned, "this was made for you."

"Put it back."

"Oh c'mon, Kate." Becky called over her shoulder. The smaller woman was eagerly working with an older, elegant-looking saleswoman, and the two of them already had their arms loaded down with clothing. "Try it on –

I'll bet it looks great on you." She turned back to her attendant. "Can you grab me one of those, too?"

"Okay…" Kate sighed through gritted teeth. Making sure that at least some reasonable clothes were included in her selections, Kate finally allowed Maria to lead her back to the dressing rooms. "See you there."

"Rrrrmph!"

The pilot was fairly sure it was Hanson who spoke from beneath a mound of walking couture.

Maria opened a walk-in dressing room for Kate, and arranged her selections strategically on hooks along the walls: coordinating separates, highlighting the eveningwear. When she was finished, the saleswoman made no move to leave. "I can handle it from here, Maria," Kate said, smiling tightly.

"No… *bella*… I help you…" She looked at Catherine, panic and doubt flickering across her face. This was simply never done.

"Really," Kate said, lightly grabbing the taller woman's bony shoulder and turning her out of the dressing room. "I'll call you if I need you."

"B – but—"

Kate slammed the door shut. "Heel, Maria," she muttered under her breath.

The pilot began picking though the draped clothes, trying to recall just which ones she'd selected in the first place. She heard the dressing room door next to her open, and from the excited chatter she could tell it was Hanson and her designer diva.

A light tap on the wall. "Kate, you over there?"

"Uh-huh." Her voice was toneless.

"Great. I can't wait to see how we look in these gorgeous things."

"I can," she mumbled.

"What?" Giggles and bumping sounds came from over the wall.

"I said, 'me too'."

Ugh. Kate shook her head, and quickly went to work. Fortunately for the tall woman, she had an unerring sense of what clothes fit her best, what caught her eye, and which were comfortable to wear. She consistently adhered to those sensibilities, rather than let herself be guided by trendy styles and high price tags.

After slipping in and out of several ensembles, Kate finally decided to splurge on three new outfits. After all, what she didn't use here, she could certainly make use of… somewhere, she rationalized. She wasn't much of a shopper, and God only knew when she'd get the chance again. She placed a white cotton three-quarter-sleeve poplin shirt over a nylon-lycra spandex tank, and a beige pencil skirt in her 'to go' pile.

Next to make the cut were a charcoal cardigan with a matching tank top, and the one pair of jeans she'd been able to find in the blasted bou-

tique. Lastly, in a concession to the spirit of
Roma, she opted for a loose-fitting white cotton
top, sleeveless, with a pair of blue patch-pocket
capri pants.

"Kate." There was a rapping on her door
this time. "Let me see."

Kate finished buttoning up her own lilac
blouse, then flung the door open to Becky. The
hawk-like Maria was anxiously hovering just
behind her.

"You no like…?" The saleswoman was disappointed.

"I like." Kate thrust her pile of selected
clothing at the taller woman. "Ring me up, sister."

Kate dropped her eyes to the young blonde
in front of her. "You look nice."

Becky was wearing a white silk and cotton
sleeveless top, with a matching lightly beaded,
knee-length skirt. "I like it too," she said. "It's
just that…" She fingered the bulky bandage that
was peeking out from beneath the shoulder strap.

Kate could see the girl's face fall. Dammit,
Hanson looked terrific in that outfit. If she
wanted it, she should get it. The tangible evi-
dence of her recent trauma would fade soon
enough. "Get it." The pilot's voice was firm.

"You think?" Rebecca brightened.

"I think." And she moved to leave the
dressing room.

"*Si.* " Becky's salesclerk jumped in. "You look adorable, darrrling," she purred.

"Hey." Becky stopped the pilot from leaving. "Didn't you try on that dress?"

"For what?" Kate sniffed. "I don't need it."

"You don't *have* to need it." Becky's eyes twinkled. "That's the joy of shopping."

"*Si,* " the saleswoman enthusiastically agreed.

God, Kate thought, *with these people the answer is always yes, if it involves a sale*. "Thought you were going to try one on?" She tried to change the subject.

"I did." Becky lowered her head, glumly. "Turns out I need to be about a foot taller to pull off something like that…"

"I get you something more petite, *bella.* " And the saleswoman scurried off.

"But gosh, Kate, if I had your… height – C'mon." The smaller woman stood tall, and grabbed the gown from the hook in Kate's dressing room. "Live a little. Try it on. You know what they say. 'When in Rome'…" She shoved the dress at Kate.

"Here you are, dear." The older saleswoman had reappeared, with a shimmering something for Becky.

"Let's go, Phillips," Becky narrowed her eyes, "or are you scared?"

Blue eyes locked on green. Catherine Phillips never backed down from a challenge, no matter *what* the circumstance. She grabbed the dress from Becky, and stuck out her chin. "Meet you in the hall."

Becky smirked triumphantly and retreated, her saleswoman in tow.

Once more, Kate undressed and, sighing, slipped the gown over her head. It was a black matte jersey-style dress with spaghetti straps. The first thing Kate noticed was that it felt wonderfully comfortable. The second thing was, as she checked herself out in the mirror, that it looked as good as it felt. Dammit, Hanson was right!

"Let's see it." More knocking on the door.

"Coming."

In her bare feet, Kate padded out into the hallway.

She was met with silence.

And then, *"Stordimento."*   'Stunning,' Becky's clerk gasped.

"Oh wow… Kate…" Becky shook her head. "Gorgeous."

"Bella… you really from Milano, no? You model there, eh?"   The haughty Maria had returned.

Other patrons in the store peeked down the hall at the commotion, catching a glimpse of the striking, raven-haired woman in the designer evening gown. The black jersey material clung to Catherine's body like a second skin, part of the reason why it felt so comfortable on her. The tanned hue of her defined arms, exposed shoulders, and plunging neckline, offered a sharp, breathtaking contrast to the midnight-black material of the dress. Down it swept, hugging every shapely curve of her along the way, finally tapering to a finish… tickling her toes.

"You have *got* to get that dress," Becky finally blurted out. Not only had she barely been able to recognize Kate in her gown, she'd been knocked for a wallop by the sheer force of the beautiful woman's sleek, panther-like presence. And Catherine Phillips was that. Beautiful.

Kate did not answer Becky right away, so taken was she by the vision she was met with in the hall. Rebecca Hanson stood there in a lightweight, coral colored, front-drape dress. It was sleeveless, but the material managed to fall over Becky's injury. The dress hung in a straight line down to just above her knees, its rayon weave lending a lustrous sheen to it.

In Catherine's eyes, the young woman fairly glowed, like a blonde goddess from ages past. "You don't look too shabby yourself," she managed to get out at last.

"You think so?" Becky twirled around for Kate's benefit. "I'll get it if you do."

"Done," Kate said, not wanting to argue. She retreated back into her dressing room before her emotions betrayed her. She leaned against the fiberboard wall, breathing heavily. *Just what the hell is going on here?* She wasn't sure she wanted to know the answer to that question.

"Now for the shoes." The pilot heard Maria go swishing off in search of matching footwear.

Take your time, Maria... take your time. Kate closed her eyes, and concentrated on steadying her breathing.

In the next dressing room down, unbeknownst to her, Rebecca Hanson focused on doing the same.

It was mid-afternoon by the time Catherine and Rebecca left the shopping district; hundreds of thousands of lire lighter, and five large shopping bags heavier. At Kate's insistence, they stopped back at the Pensione Ausonia to relieve themselves of their purchases, only to find that their travel bags had been mysteriously unpacked and their fruit and Pelligrino freshened.

Signora Canova had struck again.

The women left the *pensione* to continue their walking tour, and Kate led them on a wider sweep this time, poking their heads into a number of churches: the classic renaissance, the gilded baroque, the imposing gothic.

As they stood on the leading edge of the Ponte Cavour, a bridge crossing the Tiber, the skyline of the Vatican and the dome of St.

Peter's rose up in bold relief against a cloudless blue background.

Kate could sense the younger woman's desire to cross the river. But that would take them further from their home district, and the sun was slipping lower in the western sky. "Maybe tomorrow," Kate said, placing her hand on Becky's shoulder. "C'mon."

She directed her back down the Via del Corso, left on the busy Via del Tritone, and then straight up the Via della Stamperia to the Trevi Fountain. The travelers could hear it before they could see it – the gushing, crashing cascades of the water.

"I didn't realize it was *this* big," Becky marveled, opening the pack on Kate's back to grab her camera. She took a snap and then paused, closing her eyes and lifting her face to the fountain. "Oooh... I can feel the mist." She had to raise her voice to be heard above the roar of the fountain.

"A regular shower." Kate stole up behind her. "Here, let me take your picture."

"Would you?" Becky's green eyes blinked open happily, and she handed her the camera. "You look through here, and you press this button—"

"I think I can handle it," the pilot grinned. Becky blushed and scooted over to an edge of the fountain where the view was clear.

Kate started to frame her in the lens, when she felt a gentle tap on her arm. An elderly couple, flush from a day of touring, stood next to her. He was in Bermuda shorts, with a Nikon slung around his neck and a porkpie hat jammed on his head. She was in a designer running suit, which she'd no doubt never perspired in, wearing a belt bag and carrying a large, floral-print purse.

"Would you like my Edgar to take a picture of you and your friend?"

Kate could barely see the woman's eyes through her over-sized frame sunglasses. She'd heard about the thieves and pickpockets that seemed to be everywhere in Rome, but these two looked fairly tame.

And they were obviously, painfully American.

"Sure… sure… get over there." Edgar was only too eager to help. "I'm something of a shutterbug, you know."

"Is he ever." The wife waved a dismissive hand at her husband's behavior. "One of these days, I'm gonna KILL him," she said, laughing heartily at her own joke.

"Thanks." Kate made up her mind. "You look through here…."

Edgar studiously took in the pilot's instructions. "Got it," he said solemnly, accepting her trust in him.

Kate jogged over to Becky.

"What's that about?"

"Picture time," Kate replied, wrapping her arm delicately around the smaller woman's shoulders. Becky leaned into her, slipping her arm around her waist. Once more she was amazed at how… right, how familiar it felt to let Becky get so close. In fact, she wasn't anxious to see it end, and a goofy grin pushed her mouth up in a smile.

"Say 'cheese'!" Edgar cried, and the two women obliged him.

"Aw… that's gonna be great," the older man said, walking towards them with the camera. "You two kids look so cute together."

Reluctantly, Kate let go of Becky. "Thanks again," she said, taking the 35mm and replacing it in the backpack.

"Toodles." 'Mrs. Edgar' waved goodbye, and the couple melted off into the crowd.

"That was nice of them," Rebecca said, watching them leave.

"Mm-hmm." Catherine was digging in her pocket. "Here," she said pressing a fifty lire coin in the younger girl's hand, "toss it in."

"Oh yeah!" Becky said brightly, taking aim with her good arm towards a statue of Neptune in the frothy waters. "Throwing a coin in the fountain means—"

"That you'll return to Rome one day," Kate finished, gazing off into the roaring mists.

Becky's coin toss flew up into the sky, briefly catching the late afternoon sun, before it plummeted down, striking Neptune squarely in the nose. The sound of the hit, as well as its subsequent *plunk* into the water, was lost in the crashing eddies of the fountain.

"Nice throw," Kate said appreciatively, and she turned away.

"What about you?" Becky scampered after her. "Don't you want to throw one in?"

"I already did." The pilot lowered warm, blue eyes on her companion. "A long time ago."

They had barely scratched the surface of Rome and all it had to offer, and already Rebecca Hanson was convinced this was one of the best days of her young life, bar none. Better than her senior prom, better than her college graduation, better than the day she'd graduated first in her training class at Orbis Airlines. Not bad, for a day that had begun with her in the hospital.

If it weren't for the valleys, we'd never know it when we're standing on the peaks, the flight attendant considered, her mind skipping back to that awful hijacking.

She shuddered at the memory of how she'd been scared half out of her mind and, for the sake of her passengers, even more frightened to show it.

Just when she'd thought that things looked darkest, there was Captain Catherine Phillips, making all kinds of crazy promises that she'd get them all out of it. Alive.

And so she had.

The beautiful, dark-haired pilot had insisted on not giving up and on beating the odds, and she'd won. Her supreme confidence in that outcome had soothed Rebecca's fears, calmed her panic, until the younger woman had felt sure herself that they would make it.

Even at the end, when the hijacker had aimed his gun at Catherine, intending to fire at her as she desperately attempted to land the plane, Becky knew he would not succeed. And so she'd done her part, putting herself between the pilot and the weapon.

A popping flash, a burning pain, and then – nothing.

When she'd come to in the emergency room at Salvator Mundi, her first thoughts through the fuzzy, excited chatter around her, were of her passengers, her co-workers, and her captain.

As promised – all had made it. Calmed with that knowledge, she'd released a great, contented sigh and allowed herself to just... float away.

Later, right before she'd regained consciousness in her hospital room, she'd had the strangest dream... sensation... call it what you will. She'd been scared, frightened, lost... and then she'd felt herself being enveloped by an overwhelming aura of comfort. Protection. Love.

And then she'd heard the captain calling her crazy.

Roundly annoyed at that, *and* at Kate calling her by her last name as she did, Rebecca had awakened to see the tall, bronze-skinned woman hovering above her, holding her hand. Quickly, Kate had pulled away, embarrassed. Something in Becky had mourned the loss of that touch, of that contact, and before she'd known it, she was asking the pilot to join her for a few days of sightseeing in Rome. Even as she'd made the offer, Kate had stiffened, and Becky had instantly regretted putting her on the spot.

After all, Catherine Phillips barely knew her. Surely, she had better things to do with her time than to trail after some gimpy flight attendant all over Rome. Becky had stuck her foot in her mouth.

Again.

Just like her big brother Johnny always told her she did... spoiling surprises. Spilling the beans.

She had wanted to crawl under the sheets of her hospital bed and hide, hoping that – as if by magic – the captain would disappear.

Until she heard, "You need someone to keep you out of trouble..." and saw those blue eyes, smiling warmly.

Unbelievable. The pilot agreed to spend a few days layover in Rome with her. After all, she was planning on taking some time off, anyway. And so before she drifted off to sleep once more, Becky rested easy in the knowledge that this striking, engaging woman who'd only recently entered her life, would not be leaving it.

Not just yet.

For she found herself drawn to the taller woman's energy, to the confidence she exuded, to the safe harbor that she offered. And although in many ways Catherine Phillips was a mystery to her, she looked forward to the journey of getting to know her better. One thing was for certain; she wasn't the 'bitch-on-wings' that her colleagues had characterized her as. If only they'd had the chance to see for themselves that Kate wasn't all that bad.

Take today, for instance. Kate had been so solicitous of her, keeping an eye out for her, and yet still showing her all the sights in the area near their *pensione.* Lunch, shopping, a walking tour, the Trevi Fountain... and later, a promenade up the Via Vittorio Veneto to the beautiful Villa Borghese. The large, 17th century park had originally been built at the edge of the Porta Pinciana – one of Rome's early city gates – as the pleasure gardens for the powerful Borghese family.

They'd strolled through the lushly land-
scaped walkways; many plants and flowers were
only just beginning to bloom, and the chattering
birds in the trees sang of springtime on the wind.
Kate had asked her if she was too tired to tour
the summerhouse on the property, housing an
extensive artwork collection and several Bernini
sculptures. Of course, Becky had said 'no', and
through the museum they'd tramped, marveling
at the genius of Bernini's 'Daphne' transforming
herself into a laurel tree – twigs sprouting from
her fingertips – while fleeing from a lecherous
Apollo.

Now, Becky had to admit to herself that she
felt a little peaked as they exited the summer
house, and she hated to admit it but her shoulder
was paining her, probably due to all that clothes
shopping earlier.

"This way," Kate said, pointing to the far
end of the gardens.

Becky found that being out in the fresh air
did her good and, armed with that second wind,
she wandered with Kate through the rear gardens
to the *Pincio,* just as the sun was beginning to
set.   The terrace, an extension of the Villa,
offered a spectacular view of Rome, and the
Piazza del Popolo below.

"Oh…" Becky moved to the stone railing on
the edge of the terrace, and rested her arms on
top of it.

Kate stood by her side. "Beautiful, isn't it?"

A few clouds had spaced themselves across the sky just where the sun began to kiss the horizon, and the rays of light streaking through the atmosphere lit Rome's ancient stones and walls in undulating rosettes and ambers, as though the city itself were aflame.

Rebecca breathed deeply and shivered as the air turned crisp and cool around her, and she unconsciously moved closer to the dark woman next to her, drawn to the intensity of her heat.

"Here."

Before she knew it, her jacket had been retrieved from her backpack, and draped over her shoulders. She felt the pilot's hands linger there for a moment, before they withdrew.

"Better?"

"Yeah, thanks." Becky drew the jacket closer around her. "What a day, huh?" And she turned to look up at Kate. There, in the setting sun, the taller woman's finely sculpted features – the line of her jaw, the glitter of her azure eyes – seemed to take on an unearthly glow of their own... as if fueled by a supernatural source. Becky found herself idly wondering just what that source was... whether she'd ever be able to see it. To taste it... to touch it....

Oh God. In horror, Becky realized she'd actually started to raise her hand to the pilot's cheek. *Get a grip, woman,* she chastised herself, making a great show of slipping her arms into her jacket; fighting the flush of dismay she felt rising to her face. *I hope she didn't notice...* and matters weren't helped any when Kate moved to assist her.

"I've got it." Becky shrugged her off.

If Kate was perturbed by Becky's change in mood, she didn't show it. "How about some dinner?" she said, hoisting the backpack.

Like Pavlov's dog, just the sound of the word 'dinner' made Becky's stomach grumble. Kate heard it too, and smiled. "I'll take that as a 'yes'?"

The young blonde breathed easier, welcoming the change of subject to familiar, safe territory; she felt the blush leave her face.

"*Si.*"

Chapter
3

"Are you going to eat the rest of this?" Rebecca Hanson's hand hovered over the last piece of thick crusty bread teasing her in the basket.

"No, go ahead."

"Thanks." Becky claimed her prize and began buttering it. "This was sooooo good. Not like back home."

"Uh-huh..." Catherine Phillips pushed back from her plate, swirled a sip of red wine in her mouth, and was silently amazed at the shorthaired blonde's capacity for consumption. A large plate of antipasto, soup, a calamari dish that made Kate's stomach do flip-flops, vegetables, and fruit and cheese for desert – all had come and gone.

Not to mention, the fresh-baked Italian bread. Becky was polishing off their second basket's worth.

The girl had merrily charged through course after course, chewing and swallowing with unfettered relish. Kate had simply stuck to the antipasto and a veal chop – in spite of her companion trying to talk her into the manicotti. They had both laughed then, at the memory of how the young flight attendant had unwittingly pitched a tray of the pasta onto Kate's lap in mid-flight. The pilot was sure her regulation Orbis slacks would never be the same again.

"Mmmmm?" With a full mouth, Becky offered her a last piece of the bread.

"All yours," Kate replied, holding up a hand in surrender. Where was Hanson putting it all? Maybe the girl's appetite had been bolstered by all the walking they'd done. Surely, if she ate like this all the time, she'd be twice the size she was now. As it was, Becky's form was trim and compact, well toned and muscled, but with softness and curves in all the right places.

Kate had to know. "Do you *always* eat like this?" The question was blunt, but Becky took no offense at it.

"Well, mostly… yeah." She wiped a stray crumb from her chin. "People always tease me about it, but I do like to eat."

"Wow," Kate shook her head, "you must have a high metabolism or something."

"Maybe..." Becky took a gulp of mineral water, "but I also have to work out like a maniac, too. Lets me enjoy my guilty pleasures. How about you?" She gestured towards the taller woman. "Look at you. You're in incredible shape," she exclaimed, blushing a bit at that. "What is it? Weight training? Running? Tae-Bo?"

"Please," Kate laughed, "You're tiring me out. Actually," she hesitated, "I hardly ever work out."

"What? You're joking, right?" Becky was flabbergasted.

"Never had to, really, to stay in good shape," Kate explained. "I mean, I'm active and all, so I guess I get exercise that way. And of course, back in the Air Force Academy, we *had* to train... but no, I don't do anything now. Much."

"I hate you," Becky groaned, rubbing her eyes.

"Hey – I've just got good genes, I guess."

"Più pane?" A young, white-shirted waiter scooped the empty breadbasket and looked at Becky fearfully. The girl, while quite attractive, was eating the small restaurant into minor bankruptcy.

"Well—" Rebecca's face was thoughtful.

"No, grazie," Kate said firmly, waving the youth off.

"Prego," he breathed, relief flooding his features. He bowed and retreated towards the kitchen.

"I suppose you're right," Becky patted her stomach and smiled, gazing around the restaurant. 'Torino,' it was called. She'd heard about it from one of her fellow flight attendants on a recent haul from New York to Atlanta: reasonable prices, great food, and a good location on the Via Veneto. In the hospital, she'd vowed to Kate that she'd bring her here.

Torino had about 10 tables scattered throughout a main dining room, and a bar lined the side wall. Diners had come and gone, but it seemed to Becky that the faces at the bar never changed; Italians young and old gathered for the food, the wine, the *sigarettas* and the conversation. White tablecloths bore the faded burgundy markings of meals gone by, and the three waiters who serviced the floor spent their time either bringing food from the kitchen at a leisurely pace, or lounging casually at the bar, joining animatedly in the debates raging there.

Service had been slow and it was late, but Becky hadn't minded. And neither had the pilot across from her, judging by the way she'd seen her visibly relax as the evening wore on. But as amiable as the pilot seemed now, Becky was certain that there was still a part of herself that she kept guarded... deeply hidden, and at no small price. It took energy to stay so distant, so closed off; that's why Becky had no time for it, herself. She'd always been open and fun-loving, eager to meet people and make new friends.

And although she'd enjoyed her day immensely, she could tell those few times when Catherine withdrew. She could feel it, see it, how the angles of her face set like a stone, how her eyes grew as cold and choppy as the icy waters of the North Atlantic. Becky recalled well enough the time she'd first seen the pilot in such a state; it was back on the airliner, when the captain had sworn the hijackers would not win. When Kate withdrew to that dark place where no one else could touch her, it frightened Becky, yet she resolved to not turn away. If anything, sensing the pain that lurked there too, it only endeared the beautiful, lanky pilot to her all the more. Darn it, it would just be up to her, then, to show Catherine Phillips that there was a better way.

"So," Becky said, plunging into new territory, "wasn't there *anyone* you needed to call today? After... everything that happened?" She considered how relieved she'd been to speak to her own parents, just this morning.

"I already spoke to Cyrus," Kate said diffidently.

Cyrus Vandegrift, Orbis Airlines' Director of Flight Operations, himself a retired Air Force

Colonel, was Kate Phillips' mentor and friend. Their relationship dated back to years before at Luke Air Force Base. After the hijacking, it was thanks to her former teacher's insistence that Kate had decided to take a few days off and spend them in Rome. The fact that Rebecca Hanson figured in the arrangement had been a convenient coincidence, or so Kate tried to tell herself.

Becky could see that the older woman in front of her was tensing up, averting her eyes, but she refused to back off. "Are your parents..."?

"Dead?" Kate stiffened, and turned to stare squarely at Becky. "My father shot himself when I was twelve. My mother is still alive, but she might as well be dead for all the contact I've had with her since I left for the Academy. And," her voice grew bitter, "my little brother is dead too, thanks to an 'accident'," she used the tips of her fingers to slash imaginary quote marks in the air, "when he was flying experimental jets for the Air Force." Kate paused, her topaz eyes ablaze. "Oh, and I have an older brother too, who, I'm pretty sure hates every last stinking piece of my guts. Is that what you wanted to know?"

Kate pushed back from the table then, her eyes desperately searching the restaurant for their waiter. *Time to run again.* She spied him leaning against the bar, casually talking to a young redhead. The pilot raised her hand up, snuffling quickly at her nose along the way. *"Cameriere!"* she shouted. *"Il conto!"* 'The check!'

The waiter heard the anger in her voice, and he did not dawdle. *"Si! Si!"* he cried, scurrying back to the kitchen with a fearful look over his shoulder. He knew the stormy, dark-haired woman was not to be trifled with.

"Kate..." A voice, soft, but Kate refused to turn around, choosing instead to keep her eyes on the swinging kitchen doors. "Kate, I didn't mean – I'm sorry. I – I just..."

Catherine could hear the pain in Becky's voice. And dammit, if there was one thing she couldn't tolerate, it was Rebecca Hanson feeling badly. It just wasn't right. So, in spite of herself, Kate slowly edged around to face her companion's watery green eyes.

Kate shook her head. "It's okay," she said, reaching out a hand to lightly touch Becky's own, calming the woman. "It's not you, it's me." A heavy sigh, and she shifted uncomfortably in her chair under Becky's open, honest gaze.

"It's just... so hard for me to talk about it."

Becky thought about that. "Maybe..." she pursed her lips before continuing, "maybe it's because you *don't* talk about it."

The waiter interrupted with their check, and Kate quickly threw three 20,000 lire notes at him to make him go away.

Kate released a short burst of air, and looked at Becky. "You're right," she said simply. "I – I owe you an apology. I'm… sorry." Kate heard words that were most unfamiliar simply rolling off her tongue under the influence of this young woman.

"Apology accepted."

Kate could see the confusion and hurt ebbing away from the flight attendant's face. And with it, the guilt that she bore at having put it there.

Becky smiled, and then stretched, barely stifling a yawn.

Instantly, Kate was alarmed. What the hell had she thought she was doing, keeping the injured woman out this late?

"C'mon." The pilot picked up Becky's backpack and stood. "Let's get you to bed. Big day tomorrow."

Rebecca did not protest as the tall woman guided her to her feet, out the door, and into the crisp, cool Italian night.

Behind wispy clouds, the moon looked like a dollop of whipped cream, ready to be plucked from the chocolate midnight of the sky overhead. Traffic still buzzed along the streets, though it was not nearly so congested as earlier, and the pedestrian traffic was reduced too, with just a few couples strolling along either side of the Via Veneto.

Kate and Becky walked slowly back towards the Pensione Ausonia, taking their time, talking. A barrier neither one had been fully aware of had burned off like a warm spring shower, and the conversation flowed easily. Comfortably.

Becky told Kate how although she'd enjoyed the course-work she'd taken for her business management degree from UCLA, it was her minor in literature that she'd loved even more. Even though her parents had hoped that she'd follow her father and older brother's foot-steps into the world of finance, Becky had fancied for a time that she would be a writer, journeying to different worlds through her mind's eye, living the excitement and mystery that she might find there.

In a decision that shocked her family – and Becky most of all – she'd compromised and cho-sen to pursue a career as a flight attendant with Orbis Airlines. The people, the travel, the adventure – and maybe, someday, she'd find the time to work on that great novel.

"You'll be sorry, Rebecca," her father had warned, concerned that his daughter was wasting her not insignificant business talents on a dead-end job. But his attitude only served to fuel her desire, and Becky had attacked her job at Orbis with everything she had, never looking back. As a result, she'd ratcheted up through the ranks at the airline, scoring the preferred routes unusual for one so young. It was how she'd come to be on the hijacked transatlantic flight in the first place.

From what Catherine had heard through the grapevine about the small blonde walking next to her, she had deserved every bit of that success. Her actions on the hijacked plane had proven that beyond doubt.

Kate, in turn, described to Becky the solitary life she led in New York – her home base. She'd chosen that location not because of its close proximity to the Irish mother and Greek/Irish brother in Queens she never saw, but simply because it was convenient to JFK Airport and La Guardia. Becky's heart reached out to the pilot when she talked about her Manhattan high-rise, how the apartment was simply a place to eat and sleep – nothing more.

"Don't you ever get out and… you know, have some fun?" Becky asked.

The pilot quirked an eyebrow at her. "I don't need to have fun," she replied, planting a tongue firmly in cheek.

The two women passed through the Piazza Barberini, stopping briefly to admire the lines and form of Bernini's graceful Tritone Fountain.

"That 'Bernini' guy's everywhere, isn't he?" Becky laughed, moving closer to Kate as she did so.

"You ain't seen nothin' yet," the pilot grinned back at her. "Just wait until tomorrow! C'mon now," she smiled, moving the younger girl along.

"Eese late... too late for Miss Rebecca." The omnipresent Signora Canova shook a thin finger at them as they entered the quiet, darkened lobby of the Ausonia. "She need her sleep."

"We'll try and do better tomorrow," Kate said, quickly shunting Becky into the elevator.

"What was that supposed to mean?" Becky's voice was suspicious as Kate pulled the gate closed.

"Ahhh..." the pilot hesitated, and the ancient elevator rattled and groaned as it made its way to the fifth floor. "I think she knows you're... a celebrity."

"WHAT?"

"No big deal." Kate put a hand on Becky's arm, trying to calm her. "I just... saw her looking at the newspaper this morning. There were pictures..."

"Oh God," Becky groaned. "I think I'm gonna be sick." She leaned back against the back of the elevator car. A pause, and then green eyes blinked up at her. "So... how did I look?"

"Cute as a button," the pilot rumbled, smirking, as the elevator clanged to a stop.

It had been a long day, longer than Kate had intended, and it was obvious to her now that Rebecca Hanson was exhausted.

Truth be known, she was feeling it herself.

Too tired for words, the women silently entered the ornate room and began to ready themselves for bed. Kate kicked off her shoes and headed towards the curtains blowing gently in the breeze. She noted along the way that the canopied bed had been turned down by the *signora*. She smiled to herself, and chose to leave the window open a bit; she'd always enjoyed the sensation of fresh air around her as she slept.

"Okay with you if I keep this open?"

Becky poked her head in from the bathroom. "Sure, I like it." She had traded her jeans for a green pair of sleeper shorts, and was holding a matching top to her chest, covering herself. Kate could clearly see the bandage on her shoulder, and the packet of gauze she held in her free hand.

"Here, let me help you with that." She started moving across the room.

"That's okay," Becky ducked back into the bath, "I can do this—"

"One-armed?" Kate said skeptically. "No way. If you hurt yourself, your Nurse Ratched will have my head." And at that, she directed the smaller woman to the lidded commode.

"Sit."

Becky complied; secretly glad to let the pilot take over. Working one-handed was tough enough, and... well... not that she was squeamish or anything but... "Ah!"she gasped as Kate removed the bandage.

"Sorry," the tall woman replied, her blue eyes full of concern, "did I hurt you?"

"Well, a little," Becky replied, and while that was true, it was equally true that the feel of the woman's warm fingers against the smooth skin of her shoulder had startled her.

"Ssssh..." Kate said, softly. "This won't take a moment." Gently, she swabbed the grime of the adhesive clear, taking care to keep the entrance and exit areas of the wound dry, as the doctor had advised.

Lightly, she traced a finger on the undamaged skin adjacent to the stitched area just below the tip of Becky's collarbone, berating herself once more for the dangerous risk the girl had taken on her behalf. "This looks pretty good, considering." Her voice was quiet.

"Yeah?" Becky croaked, quickly clearing her throat. She dared not catch Kate's eye for fear that her emotions would betray her. If she didn't get a grip on herself soon, she would end up looking like a fool.

The pilot laid a fresh strip of gauze over her shoulder, securing it, front and back, with the surgical tape. "Feel okay? Not too tight?"

"Fine."

Kate stood back, admiring her handiwork. "One more thing," she said, and exited the bathroom, giving Becky a chance to catch her breath. She returned a few moments later with a glass of mineral water.

"Here."

She held out a hand containing a small, white pill. "Take this."

"Do I have to?"

"Don't argue with Doctor Phillips," Kate laughed. "It'll help with the pain *and* with sleeping."

"Sleeping will *not* be a problem," Becky yawned, taking the proffered pill and washing it down with the Pelligrino.

"Thanks."

"You'll be okay from here?"

"Okay." Becky smiled faintly. She watched the pilot leave, already missing her touch. The young woman continued to sit there for a moment, under the bright fluorescent lights of the bath, gazing morosely at the tiled floor. *No... things are definitely NOT okay...* She clutched her nightshirt to her chest, and wondered just what the hell she was going to do about it all.

Several minutes later, after Becky had composed herself, she left the bathroom to find

Catherine Phillips staring at the contents of the closet, with her hands on her hips.

"What's up?" Becky trundled slowly to the bed, finally giving in to her exhaustion, letting the numbing, soothing sensation of that 'whatever' pill creep through her system.

"I need something to wear." A voice muffled, coming from the closet.

"Can't find anything?" Becky sat on the bed and yawned, pulling a clean sheet and fluffy beige comforter on top of her.

"No." A dark head turned and faced her. "I mean, I don't *have* anything."

"Oh." Becky felt a flush rise to her face, as she got the pilot's drift.

"I could have gotten something today, if only I'd thought about it," Kate explained, "but since I normally travel alone, it's not an issue."

"Of course," the blonde hastily agreed, running a hand through her feathered hair. She forced her muddled mind to think fast. How much of this torture was she supposed to endure? "Um... why don't you check the bureau? I have a sleeper t-shirt. Signora Canova probably put it in there." And with that, she collapsed back onto a downy pillow.

Eyes closed, she heard the pilot rummaging through the drawers. "Bugs Bunny?" Her voice was incredulous.

Becky smiled. "Hey, don't knock it 'till you've worn it," she said. "You ought to try the Warner Brothers store sometime."

"I don't *think* so," Kate said pointedly.

"Take it or leave it." Rebecca heard an exasperated sigh. There was more shuffling and grumbling, and the door to the bathroom clicked shut. Apparently, Kate had chosen the former option.

Becky lay there, floating on the softness of the bed. She listened to the night sounds of Rome filtering through the window, and with each slowing breath, found herself drifting off into that hazy plane of existence which lies somewhere between full wakefulness and sleep.

"I feel ridiculous."

Becky blinked open an eyelid. There was the pilot standing before her in the moonlight, wearing – what amounted to on the taller woman – a Bugs Bunny mini-dress. It barely fell to the top of her shapely, muscled thighs. Becky decided to open both her eyes after all.

"Don't let Maria see you in that," she said, referring to Kate's high-fashion sales clerk from earlier in the day. "Or next season everybody will be wearing it."

"Uh-huh." Another sigh. "Look, are you sure you don't want me to take the sofa—"

"Remember what I said," Becky growled, moving to get out of the bed herself.

"Okay... okay." Kate lifted the blankets and eased down next to the smaller woman. She preferred a firm mattress normally, but she had to hold back a gasp of surprise at how wonderfully delightful the soft, four-poster bed was. As she put her head back on the pillow and stared up at the canopy, she could've sworn she was lying on a cloud.

There was silence for a few moments, disturbed only by the rapid pounding of Catherine's heartbeat, though she dared not allow herself to consider the reason why... that it might have something to do with the young flight attendant slumbering only inches from her. What a day.

"G' night, Kate..." A soft, breathy voice, slurred by sleep and the effects of the painkiller.

"Good-night," the pilot replied, in rich, low tones. "Sweet dreams."

There was no response from Becky, save for the deepening, evenly measured sounds of her breathing.

Though tired to the bone, it was some time before a pair of blue eyes winked shut against the darkness.

Chapter
4

Catherine Phillips was a light sleeper. Always had been, ever since she was a child, when she would awaken to the sounds of fighting. Like clockwork, it was bound to erupt on those late nights when her Greek father would stumble home drunk from a neighborhood *taverna*, where he'd spent his time since closing up the family's storefront eatery for the evening.

Her brothers slept through it all, but not Katie. On those nights, she would hear the tall, dark father she loved railing against the injustices that had been done to the immigrant Phillipi family. How a run of the bad luck had plagued them ever since the day his father,

Stavros, had hit the pebbled shores of Ellis Island and had his surname anglicized.

And it was on those nights, too, that Catherine's blue-eyed, redheaded mother, Meghan Margaret Doyle Phillips, swore that the only luck *she* believed in was in her own great misfortune at ever having married the handsome Nicholas Phillips in the first place. At ever having believed she could be happy with the man. Young Katie would press her pillow over her ears, struggling to block out the sounds of their battles, until finally they faded away of their own accord.

With the next day's dawn, it would be a toss-up whether there would be sullen, strained silences between her parents, neither willing to catch the other's eye; or if she might find her mother floating through the kitchen as she prepared the morning meal. On the good days, her mother would share slight smiles with her father; she would giggle like a schoolgirl as Nicholas reached out and grabbed her by the waist, pulling her to him.

The pattern of arguing and peacemaking continued incessantly, until one dark night, with sudden and absolute finality, Katie knew there would be no 'morning after'.

As young Kate grew up, staying on her 'edge' served her well. She was able to put in long hours studying in high school, and she never required as much sleep as her fellow cadets did at the Academy. Later, as she drew one plum assignment after the other in the Air Force, sleep seemed more a nuisance to her than anything else.

It wasn't until her little brother Brendan died, in that awful prototype F-16 crash out at Edwards, that sleep became a friend to her. For it was only then that the aching loss of the fair-haired boy, who'd wanted to be just like his big sister, eased its burden on her heart. And after she'd run away, quit the Air Force and allowed Cyrus to talk her into a job with Orbis, she'd turned that pain into a living, breathing part of herself. Stoking her fires, fueling her energy. Never letting anyone get close enough to hurt her that way again.

She was always on her guard.

It was one of the benefits of being a light sleeper.

Catherine's eyes flew open. There it was again – a horrific, grinding sound that must've been what originally loosened Morpheus' hold upon her. The pilot's senses were on full alert now, and she jolted upright in bed, attempting to ascertain the threat.

Was it the aged elevator… finally breathing its last gasp and plummeting to the *pensione's* lobby? Or was it an intruder, preying on tourists, trying to make his way into the room via the balcony doors?

"Grrrrrzzzzz-pffft-zzsssh!"

Fuck. There it was again. Her heart was pounding like a racehorse. It was close – too close! It seemed the entire bed was shaking... By God, the thing had to be right next to her. It... it was—

"Grrrzzzzz-pfffffttt!"

Rebecca Hanson.

"Grrrzzzzzzz-pffft-zzzsss!"

Snoring. Lying flat on her back, mouth wide open, sawing away like there was no tomorrow.

"Jesus Christ," Kate cursed, trying to slow down her breathing to something approaching a normal level. She eased back on her elbows, and released a soft, nervous laugh. The petite blonde hadn't been exaggerating earlier when she'd threatened Kate with her snoring. The pilot had never heard anything like it before. It was enough to wake the dead and make them buy real estate in the next town over.

She turned to glance out the window. The sky was still a midnight blue; Kate estimated that dawn was at least another hour or two away. She reached for the wristwatch she'd left on the bedside table, and pressed the light.

0400 hrs. *Great, if Hanson doesn't cut out this snoring...* "Rebecca," Kate hissed, lightly jiggling her good shoulder.

"Grrrzzzzzz-pffffttttt!"

"C'mon, knock it off." She tried nudging the woman again.

"Ngggggh." Becky turned over on her right side, facing Kate, flinging her arm squarely across the taller woman's middle.

The snoring stopped.

Now here's a predicament, Kate thought. Once again, the touch, the feel of the young flight attendant on her was so easy, so comfortable to just... go with. How much she wanted to, she considered, admiring Becky's golden hair in the moonlight. The pilot fought with her conscience, calling upon her sense of discipline. It wasn't right. Not really.

She gently tried to lift the arm away.

And Rebecca moaned, as though she'd hurt her. Uh-oh. And it was that bum shoulder, too. *It's for medicinal purposes only,* Kate told herself. She let Becky's arm drop back down.

The young woman sighed, contented with this outcome even in her sleep – and scooted closer to the tanned, rigid woman lying next to her. With a soft sigh, Rebecca crossed one of her smooth calves over the top of Kate's leg.

Oh, shit.

Becky's breathing was now whispery-light, unencumbered, and silence once again reigned throughout room number two of the Pensione Ausonia.

Catherine Phillips simply lay there, gazing at this innocent by her side, unsure whether to pray for dawn to arrive soon – or that it never come at all.

Rebecca Hanson was having that dream again. The one she'd been having a lot lately, where she was hopelessly lost, and then found. Where she was threatened... scared, and then protected, calmed. Moving from the darkness of the abyss into the Promised Land. How warm and wonderful it felt to be there. She could sense the wind blowing through the trees; hear the songbirds trilling.

Becky didn't open her eyes, not at first. Instead, she simply reveled in her surroundings, drinking in the sensations. Yes, the birds were singing, and she could feel a light breeze from the window caressing her exposed skin; a delicious contrast to the warmth she felt as she snuggled under the fluffy comforter. She felt the slight tug of an ache in her legs – not unexpected. Probably due to all that walking yesterday. Nothing a warm soak in the tub wouldn't cure. Her shoulder... well, that was still sore, but not nearly as bad as it had been. A rumbling in her stomach told her that it must be time for breakfast.

But her foggy head still felt so comfortable against her pillow, and she was so cozy where she lay, that she thought another forty winks or so wasn't entirely out of the question.

So warm. Funny, how even though she knew her arm did not rest against her body, it was not chilled. Indeed, it seemed to be heated as if from below...

With a gasp, Becky snapped open her eyes.

Oh...How embarrassing. Somehow, in the course of the night, she'd ended up pressed against the slumbering form of Catherine Phillips. In the early morning light trickling through the window, Becky found herself actually resting in the crook of the older woman's shoulder, with one arm thrown across her waist. And with a gradually dawning sense of mortification, she didn't even want to *think* about where her leg was at the moment.

Becky gulped hard. She was awake now, all right. But how was she going to extract herself from her current entanglement, without rousing her bedmate? More to the point, her body was sending her all sorts of pulsing signals instructing her to remain just where she was.

No... she groaned to herself. What would the pilot think of her?

Carefully, cautiously, she took a deep breath and began to lift her arm away.

And instantly, a dark head turned and two piercing blue eyes captured her. "Oh, you're awake."

Busted! "Ah..." Rebecca fought against the involuntary flush rushing to her cheeks, and she bolted upright in the bed. She coughed, buying herself some time.

"You okay?" Kate edged herself up on one elbow, concerned. "How are you feeling?"

"Yeah, ah... fine..." There was no getting around it; surely Kate had to have noticed. "Look, I'm sorry for... for getting all tangled up with you like that," she rushed, averting her eyes from the heat of the taller woman's gaze. "It had to be uncomfortable. You should have woken me up." She swung her feet over the side of the bed, putting distance between herself and the pilot.

"No harm done," Kate replied, grinning. "Call it self-preservation. It was the only position that kept you from snoring."

"What?" Becky swiveled around to look at Kate over her shoulder. The woman was not joking.

"Oh, no," she said, bringing a hand to her forehead.

Kate pushed herself out of the bed. "Oh yes." She padded towards the bathroom. "Can't say you didn't warn me."

"Well, if it's any consolation, I didn't hear a thing from you," Becky joked, trying to lighten the moment. She couldn't keep her eyes from following the pilot as she gracefully moved across the room. So tall, so sophisticated, and doing more for that Bugs Bunny t-shirt than she ever had.

"I *never* snore," Kate laughed. She pressed her hand against the bathroom door and stopped, swinging 'round to face Becky. "So… are you ready? For more of Rome, I mean." Her blue eyes twinkled.

Becky felt a broad smile pushing it's way across her face in spite of herself. Her green eyes sparkled. Whatever 'ailment' this Catherine Phillips had, it was catching. "I'm ready."

Under the watchful gaze of Signora Canova, the two women gobbled down a quick breakfast of some pastries, fresh fruit, rolls, and espresso. Their hostess today was featuring the same severe bun and pince-nez as she had the day before, but she had traded her floral patterned ensemble for another garish dress. This one featured a riotous swarm of day-glo butterflies, but the same jangling gold and amethyst earrings remained.

She shuttled back and forth between an alcove kitchen and the dining area, clearing the tables that must have been occupied before Kate and Becky's arrival. Periodically, she would poke her head out of the alcove, a thin *sigaretta* in hand, but she never walked through the dining room with it.

"I wonder if there's a Signor Canova?" Becky asked in a hushed voice.

"Maybe she smoked him out," Kate chuckled, daubing at her lips with a napkin. "Why don't you ask her?"

"No way." Becky's eyes grew round. "She scares me a little."

"Aw," Kate watched the older woman burst from the alcove and make a beeline for their table, "I think she likes ya."

"*Eeze* a *bello* day to see *Roma,*" the proprietress said, clearing away their empty plates. "What you sit here for? *Vanno.* Go." Her words were harsh, but there was a hint of a smile on the woman's wrinkled face, as she shooed Kate and Becky towards the door.

"Okay... okay," Kate grinned, catching Becky's eye when she hoisted their backpack. "*A più tardi.*"

"Yes... see you later," the older woman said in her low, accented voice. "You need something, you let me know, okay?" She turned to Rebecca. "Car. Picnic. Guide. *Si?*"

"Ah... *si, grazie,*" Becky said, nodding her thanks and backing into the street.

The flight attendant turned to Kate. "Wow, where did that come from?"

"The ice queen melteth," the pilot smirked, shaking her head and striking out towards the Via Condotti. "You seem to have that effect on people."

Becky answered her with a raise of an eyebrow and an impish grin. "Yeah, well, big of you to admit that, Captain," she responded as she followed after her companion.

Signora Canova was correct; the day had dawned bright and clear and temperate, unusual for Rome in early spring. Kate and Becky strolled down the cobbled walkways, soaking in the sights, breezing past the shops and cafes. The mixture of scents was intoxicating: the roasting of the beans for espresso, the mouth-watering smells from the bakeries, the *trattorias* readying themselves for the traditional main Roman meal at lunch.

Unbeknownst to the small blonde, the pilot kept a watchful eye on her, gauging her color, observing her range of motion. Rebecca did look wonderful today, well-rested and healthy, wearing one of the outfits she'd purchased the day before: a white silky sleeveless blouse, and knee-length matching skirt delicately trimmed with light beading. Kate had promised the younger woman that they'd travel farther afield today, but at the slightest sign that her companion was flagging, Kate was determined to rein in their itinerary.

As it was, Becky seemed to possess a boundless supply of energy, and it was Kate who trailed behind. No doubt due to those early morning hours she'd spent wide awake, clock-watching, while entwined in the snore-less clutches of Rebecca Hanson. The ordeal was tiring, yes, the pilot admitted to herself. But unpleasant – no. If only the young girl knew…

"This way." Kate watched Becky happily wave her towards a street-side flea market, and she obligingly followed. Something told her they wouldn't be leaving here without a slightly heavier backpack.

The market was an explosion of colors, of angry shouts and vigorous haggling, of merchants guaranteeing that their wares were the best deal in town. Or, if not, certainly better than the kiosk next door. Shoes, bags, clothing, produce, and flowers; artists and their works, soccer balls and fresh eel – all could be found within the crammed confines of the market.

Rebecca Hanson was in her element.

One grizzled flower merchant virtually accosted Becky, leaping in front of her with a bouquet of flowers.

"No... no... *grazie,*" she laughed, pushing the flowers back to him.

But he insisted, removing buds from the bouquet one at a time, reducing his price as he did so. Soon, there were half the number of flowers, and the vendor was dying a thousand deaths at the thought that this beautiful woman should spend the rest of her day without the benefit of his roses, carnations, and daises.

"Speciale. Per una bella donna. 10,000 lire."

"Really, no thanks – I don't need them," Becky protested, having exhausted her meager supply of Italian. She looked up at Kate, smiling helplessly.

The tall pilot stepped forward. Time to make a deal, she thought. Kate flipped the merchant a couple of 500 lire coins, and plucked a single rose from the bouquet. *"Affare?"* 'Deal?' Twin blue laser-beams drilled into him.

The merchant bit his lip, considering the offer. He turned his gaze from Kate to the coins in his hand, from the flower to the glowing face of Rebecca Hanson. Deciding, he dropped the lire into the front pocket of his leather apron.

"Okay," he said, bowing gallantly at Becky and bidding her farewell with a flourish of petals and greens.

"Grazie." she blushed as she passed him by. She held the bud to her nose and inhaled deeply of the aromatic scent, closing her eyes. "Mmmm… thanks, Kate."

"I didn't think we were going to get off the hook, otherwise," Kate grumbled, but secretly she was pleased at the light that just one single flower had brought to Hanson's face. For Rebecca, life appeared to be so simple, so uncomplicated. The girl, by her sweet and gentle nature, dwelled in a place Catherine Phillips could only dream of.

"Hey, look. T-shirts." Becky pulled up short in front of a table loaded down with caps and t's. "I want to get a couple for Cally and

'Becca," she said, referring to her two little nieces – her sister's children – whom she adored.

"Aren't these a little big?" Kate unfolded one and held it up. It dropped down to her knee-caps, and she recalled from a conversation they'd had on the plane that Becky's nieces were only five or six. "They'd be swimming in these things."

"Yeah," Becky said, sighing. "Maybe someplace else…" She suddenly noticed the turquoise t-shirt the pilot had grabbed. "That'd look nice on you."

"Really?" Kate thought about that. "Not that I have a death wish for Bugs Bunny or anything," she grinned.

"I wonder how much they want for it?"

Kate turned to a dark-haired young man who stood expectantly behind the table. He sensed a sale in the air. *"Buongiorno."* He winked at the dark-haired pilot.

"Quant'è?" She held out the t-shirt.

"35,000 lire," he said, folding his arms across his middle.

Oh well. Kate began reaching into her wallet for the appropriate bills. Next to her, Rebecca's brow furrowed as she did some quick math in her head.

Nearly $20.00.

"Hold it." She grabbed Kate's forearm just as the taller woman was handing over the lire.

"What?"

"Kate," she lowered her voice, "that is *such* a rip-off."

"So?" She swiveled back to the vendor.

Becky stepped in front of her, blocking the transaction. "10,000."

"Hanson…" came a throaty rumble from the pilot. What was the girl up to?

"Che cosa? Impossibile." The young vendor rocked back on his heels under the steely, green-eyed glare of this unexpected threat. He saw his sale going up in smoke. "30,000," he said, thrusting out his chin.

"C'mon, Kate." Becky yanked the t-shirt from her surprised companion's grasp, and threw it back down on the pile. "Let's go. This stuff is worthless."

"No… no… no! Per favore, signorinas!" the Italian cried out. He held his hands open wide. "25,000 lire."

Becky stopped, and turned a cold eye back to him. "12,000."

"20,000."

"15,000."

"Siete insani." The vendor was clearly desperate. "18,000."

Becky picked up the turquoise t-shirt, and her face screwed up as though the material had a foul odor to it. At this point, Kate had stepped back and was simply watching the show.

"16,000."

"17,000." The young man looked ill.

Becky's eyes narrowed. "16,500. Just because you called me crazy."

"Si, si. 16,500." The vendor was gasping now. How was he to know the girl understood a bit of Italian?

"Buono." Becky smiled happily. She handed Kate the shirt, and swiped a 20,000 lire note from the pilot's hand. She proffered it to the exhausted merchant, and patiently waited while he counted out her change.

"Grazie," the young man said, not really meaning it, dismissing them with a wave of his hand.

"Phew." Kate shook her head, amazed, as they left the flea market. "They should have you negotiating that American Airlines strike."

Becky laughed. "Hey, when the call comes, I'm ready."

The two women spent the remainder of the morning exploring the great art and architecture of the Vatican; they marveled at the size and scope of the Piazza di San Pietro, another Bernini masterpiece. Mounting the great portico, they passed into the basilica of St. Peter's itself, where once again they were overwhelmed by the colossal dimensions of the place. Becky found herself deeply affected by Michelangelo's *Pietà,* the artist's breathtaking sculpture of the Madonna holding her crucified son, Jesus. The tragic beauty of the life-sized statute was displayed under bulletproof glass, a consequence of a serious vandalism attack several years before. The young blonde mourned both for the pain of a mother's loss, and for the fact that so lovely a work of art had fallen prey to the hand of violence.

Lunchtime found the women seated in a sidewalk café along the Vittorio Emanuele, munching on pizza and sipping Coca-Colas. Traffic swept by, buzzing across the Tiber and back again: Fiats, Opels, Mercedes. Buses too, together with quite a number of small, motorized scooters. The scooters were the transportation of choice for many of Rome's young people, providing the perfect solution to pressing schedules and the city's legendary traffic jams.

"That looks like fun." Becky said, pointing to a young, helmeted couple motoring by on a Vespa.

"Do you ride?" Kate could not help but notice the younger woman's wistful gaze, following the bike.

"No, but I always wanted to learn," she sighed.

Well... they still had a lot of touring to do, and Kate was no great fan of buses or cabs. If they rode... they could see more of the sights, not to mention it would be easier on Hanson, too. She'd been holding up well so far with walking, but best not to push it.

Kate swallowed her last bite of pizza, and grabbed the backpack. "Let's go."

Becky noisily drained her glass, and stood. "Where to?"

Kate grinned. "We're going to rent ourselves a scooter."

The flight attendant's mouth fell open in a silent 'Oh'. "Wow," she said at last, breathless. Becky could feel her heart pumping faster with the anticipation of it all. "Do you know how to ride?"

"Well," Kate scratched her head, and cast her blue eyes upon the speeding traffic furiously rushing along the Via del Corso, "I've got a '91 1200 Sportster stored in the basement of my building." She slipped on her sunglasses.

"A scooter?"

"Nope," her voice was detached. Understated. "A Harley."

Catherine Phillips was having more fun than anybody had a right to. With the wind in her face, Rebecca Hanson at her back, and 125ccs of classic Vespa motor scooter beneath her, the pilot was in paradise. Sprinting in and out of the Roman traffic jams on the distinctive little Vespa, Kate knew the machine was a far cry from the 1200cc Harley she had mothballed back in Manhattan, but it would do.

She was back on a bike again. That was all that mattered.

Kate loved to ride almost as much as she loved to fly, and she knew it didn't take a shrink to figure out the reasons why. Speed. Power. Control. Freedom.

And isolation. There was that, too. In her days at Luke Air Force Base in Arizona, and later, at Nellis, how she had loved to take her bike out at night and race it along the flat ribbons of darkened road, smoking any other man or machine that dared oppose her! It was then, like when she was flying, that she could clear her head. See the big picture. Challenge her demons... or run from them, if she chose.

She was proud of her bike, delighted in her own ability to dominate it. With a twist of her right handgrip, the machine would growl to life, surging with a low-end torque that packed an instant wallop. Unlike the boxy Vespa, her Harley-Davidson featured an agile, lean, street fighting design that, when combined with an open throttle on the powerful motor, made it her weapon of choice.

Hugging a curve as she gunned the engine of the scooter, Kate considered that it had been some time since she'd last had her Harley out, had allowed herself to feel that thrill. The pilot resolved that once she got home, things would change.

Maybe even Hanson would like to go for a ride sometime. She certainly seemed to be enjoying herself now. Already they'd buzzed the Circus Maximus, ancient Rome's version of a horse racing track. Afterwards, Kate had motored over to the leading edge of the Via Appia, or the Appian Way.

She'd cut the Vespa's engine there, and she and Becky had poked around for a bit.

In the warm afternoon sunshine, the sagging cypresses and umbrella pines stood guard over ruined sepulchers dating back to before the time of Caesar. The shadows of that distant past had sent an involuntary shiver through Catherine. People who once were as living and breathing as she, had dwelt on that same spot of *Vecchia Roma* – Old Rome. They'd reached out across the years to her, and she'd answered their call. Kate had actually stooped down and let her fingers trace a path along a small tract of the ancient paving.

Looking off down the road, towards the east, the Via was lined as far as she could see with tombs and fragments of statuary. She'd closed her eyes in the whispering quiet, absorbing the coolness of the stone in the sultry air. She had fancied then that she could hear the tread of triumphant Roman legions, pounding along the road. The image was so real, so vivid, that she'd found it a bit... unsettling.

She'd popped open her eyes, to see Becky looking at her strangely.

"You okay?"

"Fine," Kate said, forcing a smile to her face. She brushed off the knees of her new blue Capri pants. "Let's go."

Heading back into the city, taking a course along the Tiber, Catherine was forced to slow their speed down somewhat as they'd motored through the narrow streets of one of Rome's oldest neighborhoods: the *Trastevere*. There, they'd jounced along cobbled stones; past grocery stores, dusty artisans' workshops, and residences crazily stacked in tottering buildings, festooned with washing hung out to dry.

Afterwards, they'd flown by the Vittorio Emanuele II Monument, sitting squatty along the Piazza Venezia, looking for all the world like a gigantic wedding cake. The marble structure housed Italy's Tomb of the Unknown Soldier and eternal flame.

Now they were heading to Rome's ancient marketplace – the Forum.

Traffic was heavy as she climbed the scooter uphill towards the *Monte Palatino,* or the 'Palatine Hill', yet Kate hated to throttle back. Dammit, they were so close; to slow down now didn't make any sense.

"Kate, I really don't think you should go around that bus…" The voice of Rebecca Hanson was half carried away on the wind, yet Kate could feel the heated tickle of it in her ear as she maneuvered the Vespa past the rear edge of the *piazza.*

"No problem," the pilot tossed back over her shoulder. Traffic was going entirely too slow for her tastes, but that was part of the fun, the challenge of not having to cut her speed while at the same time threading her way through the cars, buses, and opposing scooters.

Not to mention those pedestrians foolish enough to venture into her path.

A black Renault shot out from the Via del Corso, hurtling towards the square, collapsing Kate's intended route past the lumbering tour bus. *"Kate!"* Becky's voice was a giddy shriek. She'd seen the Renault, too. Kate felt a squeeze as Becky tightened her hands about her waist; felt a shifting of the younger woman's skirted thighs as they tensed behind her.

To the casual eye, it appeared as though they would never make it.

To Catherine Phillips, there was never a doubt they wouldn't.

The pilot cut the Vespa loose, gunning the motor for all it was worth. The bike hiccupped for a moment, and then leaped forward, its engine buzzing like an angry honeybee. The speed was there.

The only problem was, as Becky saw it, that they were hurtling directly towards the on-rushing Renault.

"Aaah!" Becky ducked her head into Kate's shoulder. She was going to die – she just knew it! So why did it seem to her, from the rumbling vibration she felt throughout the pilot's torso, that the woman was actually... laughing?

The Renault's driver sounded his horn in a furious staccato burst.

"Hey – you jerk!" In the midst of her maneuvering, Kate took the time to hit the little 'hooo-gah!' horn of the Vespa. Not quite the intimidating blast she'd been counting on, but it would do.

Kate never wavered in her course, mentally plotting a line that would take them – just – between the car and the bus. "Hang on!" she cried to Becky.

No problem. Becky gripped the pilot tightly.

The car was speeding closer.

The creeping tour bus, with exhaust pluming from a rear tail pipe, suddenly started to accelerate.

And the driver of the Renault finally blanched. With a *screeeeech!* he at last swerved to his right, angrily giving way.

"Ha!" Kate laughed, satisfied. Without having to check her speed in the least, she nimbly zipped between the two moving vehicles.

The car's driver was screaming at them through his open window, and Becky thought she could smell the smoke from the cigarette that dangled from his lips.

A quick right-hand turn, and then a left, cutting across traffic, and the pilot drew the Vespa to a stop in an area outside the Forum already congested with parked scooters.

"Ohhh…" Becky leaped off the back of the bike, her knees knocking, whipping her helmet off. "KATE!"

"Hey – we had the right-of-way." The taller woman eased herself from the seat, unbuckling her helmet and swinging her long, ebony hair free. "Besides, he wasn't gonna hit anybody."

"How do you know?"

The pilot took off her sunglasses, folding them into the pocket of her white, sleeveless blouse. "I *know,*" Kate said, merriment dancing in her eyes. "You were scared, weren't ya?"

"No, I wasn't," Becky said primly, settling her helmet on the bike and grabbing her back-pack.

"Were too." Kate easily stripped the pack from her, swinging it onto her shoulder.

"Was not," Becky insisted, and then, catching the grin on the Kate's face, she began to chuckle sheepishly. "All right," she admitted, striking out towards the Forum entrance, "I was scared shitless, okay? Feel better?"

"Well, you needn't have been." Kate fell in next to her. A moment's hesitation, and then, "You know I'd never do anything to hurt you, Hanson." The pilot tried to keep her voice light, unconcerned, but Becky caught the hint of seriousness in her tone.

They had reached the stone and brick entrance of Rome's ancient marketplace. Becky stopped, and looked up into two sky-blue eyes that were watching her carefully, appraisingly.

"I know."

Surrounded by the buildings and highways of modern Rome, the Forum was an anachronism of starkly impressive proportions. The white light of direct sunshine reflected off of the marbled columns and statues, and they throbbed with life in the long-dead square. Some of the ruins were still standing; more were lying askew as though tossed about by a titan's child.

Kate looked out over the ancient gathering place, and it was easy to imagine it filled with immense, brightly painted temples and stately, extravagant shops, lorded over by emperors living in their palaces on the Palatine.

"Rome was built on seven hills, you know," Becky said, as they walked among the tumbled-down stones.

"Mm-hmm…"

"Yeah." The young blonde chose to ignore the pilot's apparent disinterest. "Legend has it that the twins Romulus and Remus were abandoned as infants, suckled by a she-wolf on the banks of the Tiber, and then finally adopted by a shepherd."

"A shepherd." Kate's voice was flat.

"Well, after they were encouraged by the gods to build a city, the twins chose this site, fortifying it with a wall you can still see on the Palatine." Becky shielded her eyes against the bright sun, and gazed up at the hill. "During the building of the city, the brothers quarreled, and in a fit of anger Romulus killed Remus!"

"You don't say."

"Hey." Becky poked Kate in the ribs.

"Sorry," Kate said, laughing.

Becky dramatically cleared her throat before she continued. "Even to this day, it is said that the twin brothers guard the fortunes of their eternal city."

"Well." Kate clapped her on the back, letting her hand linger for a moment. "Didn't realize you were such a storyteller."

"Actually," Becky blushed, "I am. In college I was part of a group called 'The Story Painters'. Just me and a bunch of my friends." She scuffed at a loose stone as they walked. "We'd dress up as house painters and go around to visit kids. You know, at schools and hospitals and stuff, telling children's stories. Putting on little plays."

"Wow," Kate said, impressed. "Sounds like it was fun. Bet the kids loved it."

"Oh, they did." Becky turned to her, green eyes bright and shining. "But I did too. Just as much."

Kate turned away from the young woman's gaze, but her voice was soft, hopeful. "You'll have to tell me one of those stories, sometime."

"Ah... it's just kids' stuff."

"No," Kate said earnestly, spinning back to Becky. "Really. I mean it. I'd like to hear one."

"Well." Her face lit up. "There was this *one* story about a rabbit and a hedgehog..."

Rebecca Hanson was off and running, spinning her fable about the rabbit with prickly fur and the hedgehog that lost its quills. Catherine enjoyed the sound of her companion's voice, rising and falling, assuming the different tones of the characters: one voice deep and husky, another, high and querulous.

The two women left the Forum and crossed the street into the Colosseum; to the pilot, the circular edifice looked for all the world like an ancient Yankee Stadium.

"And so the rabbit saved the poor hedgehog from the evil fox..."

Before she even knew what was happening, the tall, dark pilot found herself being mesmerized by the familiar, comforting hum of Becky's voice. Falling under her spell. The timbre of it was like sweet nectar, drawing her in.

Fuck, Kate thought, still in denial. *It can't be the damned rabbit story.* By now, they stood on a platform on the upper level of the Colosseum, overlooking the arena. Becky had finished her tale, and had moved on to the history of the monument; how it once seated over 50,000 spectators, and featured shaded awnings made from the sails of ships.

"Uh-huh."

Kate was listening with half an ear; casting her eyes distractedly around the aged walls. Something about the place was making her uneasy. Perhaps it was the crumbly condition of the stones, or else the knowledge of the horrific suffering and death that had taken place there, all in the name of sport. Additionally, a tourist bus must have arrived, for now a crowd was closing in behind them, pressing her closer to Becky.

Still, the flight attendant kept chattering away, snapping pictures.

The pilot stood directly behind Becky now, crushed into place by the tourists, while the smaller woman leaned on the railing in front of her, happily taking in the sights. Kate looked down upon the golden head, breathed in deeply of the calming, soothing spring-rain scent of the girl, and she knew she either had to get the hell out of there now, or else reach down and pull her close and...

"Why don't I wait for you outside?" Kate started to push her way out of the crowd.

"Huh?" Becky spun around, mystified.

"Too crowded for me up here," Kate said, and that much was true. "There's a stand on the corner where you can get your nieces those t-shirts and miniatures... I'll wait for you near there, okay?" She offered her companion a thin smile.

"Well… if you're sure… I want to take just a few more pictures."

"Great," Kate gulped. "See you there." Then she bolted.

Phew, she thought, sucking wind as she ducked into the cool, enclosed concourses of the arena. She wound her way down to street level and burst out into the bright sunshine, not quite free of the smothering trepidation that dogged her.

She eased herself down onto a cement coping that ran along the exterior of the Colosseum, about halfway between the arena and the street. The souvenir stand was about 30 yards away. Kate fought to clear her mind, struggled to settle the pounding of her heart, but try as she might to summon that serenity, it would not come.

What the hell was she thinking of? Looking at Rebecca Hanson… *that* way.

Over the years, she'd taken her share of men to her bed, and women, too, when the opportunity presented itself. She'd never bothered to form relationships, never wanted to. She could admit to herself that she'd used her partners simply to get what she wanted, in a purely physical, needful way. Nothing more.

NEVER anything more.

The back lot of a darkened bar. A tumbled apartment whose address she had no reason to recall. Napkins with phone numbers scrawled on them she'd balled up and thrown away. Nameless. Faceless. Empty. Oh, she knew about sex all right. More than most. But love... what a pipe dream. She had no time for it.

A blonde, emerald-eyed, smiling face popped in to her mind's sight.

Dammit.

She had to get her act together. For the young woman's sake, as well as her own, Rebecca Hanson was a complication she simply couldn't afford.

"Hey!"

Catherine Phillips nearly leaped out of her skin.

"Sorry. Didn't mean to scare you."

"I wasn't scared," the pilot said gruffly. "Ah... did you get your pictures?"

"Yeah." Becky reached for the backpack containing her wallet. "Let me go get those souvenirs for Cally and 'Becca."

"Okay," Kate said, unmoving.

"Uh... you'll wait here?"

"Sure," the pilot replied, and she watched Becky wade off towards the stand. The sidewalks in front of the Colosseum were packed full of tourists, business people, and a group of rag-tag youths who Kate fancied ought to be in school. She couldn't blame them, really, not on such a gorgeous day. There was a crowd by the souvenir stand, too, and so Kate was happy to put some space between her and Rebecca for the moment. She sighed heavily.

Breathe…

Becky idly picked up and put down t-shirt after t-shirt, much to the consternation of the merchant behind the stand. He trailed in her wake, re-folding each one back to his original specifications. He would've chased her off by now, if she hadn't already selected two metallic miniatures of the Colosseum for purchase. She was a buyer, not a window-shopper. That, and the fact that she was the most beautiful girl he'd seen all day, gave him patience.

The flight attendant could not decide. The prices were right – it wasn't that. It was just… her mind kept skipping back to that moment upstairs, in the arena. She could feel Kate behind her, the heat of her, so near, and suddenly the woman had closed off, withdrawn. Becky knew that distancing look well by now.

The pilot had literally run away, and even now preferred to lounge on the concrete rail rather than join her for some shopping. Had she done something to offend her? Rebecca wracked her mind, but she couldn't come up with a thing.

On the contrary, their afternoon together had been thrilling. Flying all over Rome on the back of Kate's scooter, the exciting whip of the wind against her exposed skin, her arms around the pilot's solidly muscled waist… Becky blushed at the thought of how she had enjoyed every stolen moment of it.

O God… What if her feelings were too obvious? What if Kate had noticed? Even now, she missed having the tall, silent woman near. Dammit, how could she ever hope the pilot would understand, when she couldn't even explain it to herself? At times she felt so confused, so mixed up over what she was feeling, and then Kate would turn those blue eyes towards her, smiling, and for the briefest of instants, Becky would experience an agonizing flash of clarity. Of understanding. Of what was right.

And then it would slip away, just beyond her reach.

Rebecca Hanson did not take relationships lightly, she never had. Oh, she'd dated plenty throughout high school, college, and beyond, gotten serious with a few of her boyfriends; even thinking she was in love once or twice. But, looking back on it now, she knew it wasn't true. They'd been wonderfully nice, and she'd certainly cared for them, but the affairs had always sputtered out, after a time.

She wasn't disappointed, not really, chalking it up to life experience. Although the physical aspects of those relationships – *it was the sex, Becky,* she thought – left her vaguely dissatisfied. Wistfully yearning for something more.

"Signorina!" The souvenir vendor's plain-
tive plea roused Rebecca from her daydreams.
"Which you like, eh?"

The white ones in front of her, sporting the
Italian flag on the front, would be fine for the
girls. "Two of these," Becky said, unzipping the
backpack for her wallet.

Ah, well.

Love.

Skyrockets and pinwheels. It was out there,
waiting for her someday, she was sure of it.
When the right person came along...

A shout, while at the same time, the backpack was wrenched from her hands. She felt a
sharp shove to the middle of her back, and then
Rebecca Hanson's world was spinning, and she
was falling—

"Gotcha."

Two strong arms, plucking her out of mid-
air. Propping her up on her feet. Blue eyes raking over her, full of concern. Skyrockets and
pinwheels. Catherine Phillips had saved her –
again.

"You okay?"

"Yeah," Becky said breathlessly, bending
over with her hands on her knees. What the heck
had happened? Quickly, she got her answer.

Two young men, little more than boys,
really, were trying to get away through the
crowds, one tightly gripping her backpack.
They were dark-skinned with jet-black hair, and

wore washed-out gray t-shirts, dark pants, and over-sized basketball shoes.

Kate Phillips was a blur of motion. In three quick steps, she caught up to the youth with the backpack. She grabbed him by the scruff of his neck, and he dropped the bag, thinking it would distract her. Frantically, he tried to break away. His compatriot, seeing he'd been snared, hit the afterburners and disappeared. No matter. The pilot had the one she wanted.

She scooped up the pack one-handed, never letting go of the boy. Angrily, she swung him around, seizing the front of his t-shirt, slamming him with stunning force against the end of the souvenir stand.

The kiosk rattled as though it had been hit by an earthquake.

"Voi poca parte di shit." 'You little piece of shit.' Kate snarled, *"Provare ancora quello e li ucciderò con le mie mani nude."* She tightened her hold around his collar, and her voice was low and threatening. *"Capisce?"*

"Si! Si!" Wild eyes bobbed 'yes' in understanding.

"Vanno." Kate released the youth with a shove. He nearly lost his footing before he was able to scramble off, casting a furtive look back over his shoulder.

Her face dark with anger, Kate wordlessly handed the backpack over to Becky, oblivious to the astonished buzz of the surrounding crowd.

"Thanks," Becky said at last, with a hollow laugh, reaching once more for her wallet to complete her purchases. She hesitated, her eye catching a splatter of red at her feet.

Her rose.

It must have fallen from her backpack during the assault, and been crushed underfoot on the hot concrete. Becky's stomach did a flip-flop. She looked up, following the pilot's gaze across the Via Imperiali; her companion was still attempting to track the would-be thieves. "What did you tell him, anyway?"

Pale eyes turned a cloudy gray. "I told him if he ever tried that again, I'd kill him with my bare hands."

Silence.

"Oh," Becky said finally, choking. She slowly turned back to the slack-jawed vendor, picking up her miniatures and t-shirts. The pilot would kill for her. A chill ran through Rebecca, and a sadness, too. Catherine Phillips did not make idle threats.

Of that, she had no doubt.

The two women walked quietly back to the parked Vespa. Becky could see the tight lines marring Kate's features, the tense set to her broad shoulders. Any good humor the pilot might've embraced during the afternoon had evaporated.

"Are you mad?"

"No." Kate reached for her helmet.

"Are you sure? Because—"

"Hanson, I am *not* angry." The frustration in the taller woman's voice was plain. "Let's just forget about it, okay?"

"Okay," Becky said, chastened. She dipped her head morosely as she put on her helmet.

Kate noticed the look, and sighed. "It's not you," she said, coming around to the rear of the Vespa, tying on the backpack. "Those guys back there just... pissed me off, that's all."

That's an understatement, Becky thought, considering how her companion had reacted instinctively, violently, in order to protect her.

"Look," Kate turned an eye towards the western sky, "if there's nothing else you'd like to see today, why don't we think about dropping some stuff off at the *pensione* and grabbing some dinner?"

Nothing else she'd like to see? Ha! Rebecca Hanson was just getting started. "Well," she began, "there *is* one more thing that's so close... it'd be a shame not to swing by."

"What?" Kate folded her arms across her chest. She could see that Hanson was gingerly trying to snap her out of her mood, and dammit, if it wasn't working. God, she'd been so scared when she saw those young thieves reaching for the smaller woman, shoving her – she'd nearly gone blind with rage. Fortunately, no harm had been done after all. Rebecca was fine, and she'd recovered the backpack.

"I saw it in an old movie once." She lifted her eyes to the pilot and grinned. "It's called the 'Mouth of Truth'."

Kate groaned. "I know the place. It's in a church—"

"Yeah," Becky said happily, climbing on the back of the Vespa. She opened the palms of her hands expectantly. "What are we waiting for?"

Becky was right, the church of Santa Maria in Cosmedin was not far away. And, truth be known, Catherine didn't mind extending their sightseeing just a bit longer. It gave her another excuse to feel the slim arms of Rebecca Hanson gathered about her waist, hanging on for dear life.

Santa Maria was a newer church by Roman standards, dating back to medieval times. While the interior was well preserved and impressive to look at, the main draw at the site was an ancient marble mask called "La Bocca della Verità" – 'The Mouth of Truth'.

A brief scooter-ride later, and the two women's footsteps were scuffling along the lower cement portico of the church, which was deserted at this late afternoon hour. The air was cool and damp, smelling of ancient forgotten secrets, and the streets of Rome seemed far away indeed, from within the recessed, shaded columns of the walkway.

"Wow," Becky said, as they approached the age-old Tritone mask. From the great, rounded disk, a wizened face sprang forth, eyes opened wide and missing nothing; the florid image pitted and grooved by time. The mouth of the face was frozen in an open 'O', inviting the adventurous to subject themselves to its judgment.

They stopped in front of the mask, and Kate lightly placed a hand on its cheek. She turned to Becky. "In medieval days, a person put their hand in the mouth, while taking an oath. If they were a liar... swore falsely, legend has it that their hand was bitten off."

"Oooh." Becky turned up her nose distastefully.

"Care to try it?" Kate arched an eyebrow in challenge to the younger woman.

"Sure," Becky said simply, feigning a lack of concern. The sun was beginning to set, and the shadows in the cool portico were deepening. She began to lift her hand closer to the mouth.

"Careful," Kate chuckled. "You don't know *what* could be hiding in there."

Becky inhaled sharply, turning fearfully to Kate. Her hand froze in mid-air, just outside the toothless, blackened mouth. Heck, she didn't believe in those crazy superstitions. And she was basically an honest person anyway. She had nothing to fear.

Stiffening her backbone, she started to edge closer to the mouth. Okay, so maybe she wasn't being entirely truthful where her feelings for Catherine Phillips were concerned, but that didn't mean she'd lose her hand over it, right?

Becky's fingers started to tremble.

Right?

"No," Becky gasped, whipping her hand away as though she'd been burned. "You first." She laughed nervously, hoping the pilot couldn't see how unhinged she'd become. Darn it, it was just an old mask.

"Okay…" Kate said, in a voice low and ominous. It was as though she actually feared the mouth herself. "Here goes."

Slowly, the tall woman slipped a tanned hand into the darkened orifice.

The sounds of water trickling down the aged walls mingled with the tempo of the women's breathing. In the near quiet, the present slipped into the past, leaving nothing in its wake but this stony, impartial arbiter of truth.

"Aaaaah!" Catherine's face contorted in pain.

"What is it?" Becky screamed.

"I – I don't know." Desperately, Kate tried to remove her hand, but she was held fast by some unseen force within the mask. "Oh God!" she cried, pulling on her arm with her free hand.

"Kate!" Becky jumped in to help, tugging on her arm, trying to wrest her loose. Wasn't there anybody else around who could help? Her eyes desperately swung across the empty court-yard. "Pull, Kate!" she shouted frantically.

In one smooth motion, the pilot's hand popped out. She thrust it in Becky's face. "Boo!"

"Ahhhh!" Becky leaped back as though she'd been stung. "Why you—." She gritted her teeth.

Kate roared with laughter. "C'mon." She directed a shaken Becky back down the portico towards the street. "You're just mad because I gotcha again, didn't I?"

"You... you scared me, you big jerk." Becky struggled to calm her breath, to settle her fluttering heart.

"Success," Kate smirked, enjoying her companion's flushed discomfiture.

"Obviously," Becky said archly, "one of us is keeping score."

"Yeah, you'll have to let me know about that sometime," Kate blithely said, picking up her helmet and swinging astride the Vespa. She turned smiling blue eyes to the frustrated blonde. "Let's eat, shall we?"

It had been some time since the sun had set over the seven hills, but Rebecca Hanson was still at it.

Food.

Catherine warily regarded the younger woman across the table, and was forced to throw in the towel. "That's enough," she said, pushing away her plate. Kate had already enjoyed a sizable antipasto, as well as delicious pasta with a homemade tomato, bacon, and pecorino cheese sauce. Those indulgences, together with her share of bread and a bottle of Bardolino, left her feeling comfortably full.

Becky paused in her feeding, a chunk of bread already halfway to her mouth. She considered her companion's words. "Me too," she said self-consciously, putting the bread down.

Kate laughed. "C'mon, Champ. You're just getting started."

"Well," Becky eyed a tray of passing deserts, "that ricotta cake looks awfully good…"

"Go for it." Kate flagged down the waiter, and in short order Becky was happily munching on her creamy cake, while both women sipped on cappuccinos.

The restaurant, Palermo, hugged the edge of the Tiber, not far past the lighted Castel Sant'Angelo, and it was an easy walk from the Pensione Ausonia. They'd left the scooter behind since the restaurant was so close, with

Kate making sure that Becky was not overly tired from their busy day.

They had chosen to stop back at their room, drop off the backpack, and freshen up prior to heading out for dinner. As they tramped into the lobby of the *pensione,* there was Signora Canova, sitting guard behind her oak desk. She had greeted them with a smoky, wordless wave.

"I wonder if she ever sleeps?" Rebecca had whispered as they'd strolled out into the warm evening.

"*I* wonder if she's even human." Kate had chuckled softly. "She's a virtual smoke-stack."

Quickly, the women had found Palermo, and ducked in for a traditional Italian dinner among a native crowd.

"How about a little walk before we head back?" Becky asked, draining her cappuccino.

"You sure you're up for it?" Kate wanted to be certain. It wouldn't do for Hanson to exhaust herself. After all, she was still recovering.

Becky grimaced. "Don't go there," she warned. God, why was Kate still babying her?

"Okay." Kate held up her arms in surrender. "Why don't we walk along the river for a bit?"

"Oh, great," Becky replied, her frown easing into a smile. "I've always wanted to do that." *With someone I care about...* she bit her tongue before adding that last. For the young blonde it was enough that she was in the company of the tall, mystifying airline pilot.

They left the restaurant and began moving naturally towards the lights of the Castel, picking their way along a cobbled path following the Tiber.

"Nice night," Becky said, enjoying the temperate air. "Pretty wild for early April, eh?"

"Mm-hmm," Kate grunted.

Past the Castel, in the distance, the glow of Vatican City and the dome of St. Peter's stood out against the Roman skyline. Becky paused, leaning against a guardrail, and gazed out over the scene. She could feel the pilot standing behind her. Her eyes swept over the city, and she thrilled at the excitement, at the promise of it all. It seemed to pulsate with life.

"Hey, what's that?" Becky stood on her toes and pointed to the river below. Docked at the water's edge was a barge, strung with Chinese lanterns. The faint tones of music carried up from beneath a canopy in the center of it, and a number of people milled about, laughing, drinking, and dancing.

"Dunno." Kate was plainly not interested.

"Oh, come on, you." Becky grabbed her by the wrist. "There's only one way to find out." And she led the way to a gate on the path, which opened to a staircase cut into the side of the river. Obviously, it worked its way down to the barge. A laughing couple, holding hands, got to the gate ahead of them and headed down.

"What if it's private?" Kate protested.

"Well, then we'll just have to get ourselves an invitation now, won't we?" Becky disappeared over the edge.

God... With a heavy sigh, the pilot trailed after her.

As it turned out, the barge, Ciriola, was open to the public, featuring evening entertainment on Tiber, just below the Ponte Sant'Angelo. A sound system pumped Italian tunes over the water, and a bar and tables were set up around a small dance floor. Some couples swayed slowly to the music, while most of the other patrons preferred to listen, drink, smoke, and talk.

Rebecca Hanson soon found herself swept up in the exuberance of it all, as she and some newfound friends found themselves chattering away in a loose blend of basic Italian and English. She sipped periodically from a rapidly produced glass of wine, and found herself enjoying the attentions of three or four young men who suddenly found her infinitely fascinating.

Catherine Phillips stood off to one side, at the opposite end of the bar, darkly nursing a whiskey and water. Becky seemed to be having a good time, anyway, and the pilot supposed that was what mattered most.

"Kate." Becky's voice exploded in laughter. "Get over here. Listen to this story of Eduardo's."

But the pilot simply smiled faintly, and waved. Becky locked questioning eyes on her for a few seconds, but then, as Eduardo draped his arm about her shoulders, she giggled and returned her attention to her admirers.

Kate steamed. They were boys. What did they know? She swished a gulp of the cheap whiskey around in her mouth, relishing the bitter taste, before swallowing hard. Why… if she had half a mind, she'd…

A sudden commotion at the far end of the bar caught her attention.

What the hell…? A fight had broken out, between Eduardo and the rest of Hanson's fan club. The young man lunged after a taller, more muscled youth, and shoved him over the side of the barge with a splash.

Kate could see the fear skip across Becky's face, as she shrank back from the fighting. In seconds, the entire rear portion of the barge was enveloped in the wave of an all-out brawl. Becky was trapped.

"Hanson!" Kate started pushing her way madly through the crowd, dodging wild swings, fighting to get to Rebecca's side. "Over here!" She gestured towards a path of least resistance between the back of the bar and a lowered rail behind it. The area was obviously not meant for patrons, but it would provide Kate with a means of getting Hanson the hell out of there.

"Okay…" She could hear Becky's frightened voice over the shouts and cursing; the young woman kept her green eyes focused on the pilot as she tentatively worked her way towards her.

"That's it!" Kate shoved a drunken Italian aside. She was almost to her. Just a little bit more. In the distance, she could hear the whining of the *polizia* sirens. No way. She'd had enough of those people recently.

"Kate, I'm – Aaaah!"

Oh, shit! One of the brawlers had tumbled back towards the rear rail, desperately flailing his arms to maintain his balance. He did, but not before shoving an unsuspecting Rebecca Hanson headlong over the railing, splashing her into the Tiber.

"Hanson!" Kate cried out, her heart leaping into her throat.

Dumbly, the Italian turned around. He realized he'd hit something, but seeing no one there but a livid, dark-haired woman, he mumbled an apology and pushed off back into the brawl. He figured he had better odds there, rather than taking his chances against Kate.

"Rebecca!" Kate's voice was hoarse as she leaned over the low railing. Her eyes desperately skimmed the inky blackness of the waters for a blonde head.

Nothing.

Without a moment's hesitation, Catherine swung over the rail, and dove cleanly into the river near where she guessed Rebecca might be.

Though the evening Roman air had been warm, the waters of the Tiber were like an ice-bath, cinching its cold fingers around her chest, squeezing, numbing the life from her, dulling her senses. Frantically, she swept her hands around in zero visibility, clawing for something, anything that might lead her to the young flight attendant. After long moments, the pilot finally made contact with the silted river bottom, empty handed. *Dammit! Where is Hanson?*

She was panicking now; the burning pressure in her lungs told her she needed to take a breath, and soon. Mentally cursing, she pushed off awkwardly from the muddy bottom, propelling herself back toward the surface, letting the dim outline of the barge overhead serve as her guide. As she swam through the swirling water, her eyes fought to penetrate the murk, searching desperately for even a trace of Hanson's blonde hair. *Fuck – this water is cold!* Her kicks towards surface grew sluggish… it seemed so very far away. But Kate weakly persisted, knowing that if she could just steal another few breaths of air, she'd give herself a second shot at finding Rebecca.

Just when she thought her body would over-rule her mind and trick her into thinking she could draw in life from water, her dark head

broke the surface. Kate took in great, heaving
gulps of air, sputtering plumes of water from her
mouth. The roar of the blood in her head nearly
deafened her, and she tilted backwards towards
the night sky, blinking her eyes against the sting
of the dirty water. Concentrated on getting her
breath.   On re-grouping for another effort.
Where she would either retrieve Hanson, or die
trying. A few more raw gasps, and it was time.
With numb limbs she steadied herself in the
water, and began sucking in a last, deep breath,
preparing to dive.

"KATE!"

Above the throbbing crescendo in her head
and the riotous noise from the barge, she heard
it.

"Hanson?" she croaked.

"Kate, over here!"

Blearily, the pilot spun around in the water,
towards the sound of the voice.

Thank God. There was Rebecca Hanson,
hanging onto the side of a low dock at the river's
edge.

"Rebecca." Kate's voice was a whisper as
relief flooded through her, and she began pad-
dling towards the dock.

Drawing closer, she could see how round
Hanson's eyes were in the moonlight.

"Good God, Kate." Becky's voice betrayed
a mixture of anger and fear. "What the hell did

you think you were doing?" She reached a hand out to the pilot, pulling her to the side.

With her last bit of strength, Kate boosted Becky out of the water, minding her shoulder, and then heaved herself onto the wooden dock.

There was silence for a moment, as the two women simply lay there in the darkness, dripping; catching their wind, slowing their hearts.

"I – I saw you go in," Kate rasped at last. "I couldn't find you. Couldn't hear you."

Becky levered onto her elbows. "That's because I landed closer to this dock, and I happened to be busy spitting out water when I saw you go flying off the back of the barge like a madwoman."

"It's called a 'rescue'," Kate said sharply, edging herself up on one arm, shivering. "You're welcome."

"When you were gone for so long…" Becky lowered her eyes. "I got worried."

"What can I tell you?" The pilot sat up the rest of the way, her breathing still ragged. Surely, she should have gotten her wind back by now. "I thought you were still down there."

"I was up here, waiting for *you.*"

Kate coughed, and thought about that for a moment. She snuffled at her nose before continuing. "Well. Considering the alternatives… I'm glad you were." She turned to face the smaller woman and held out her hand, pulling her up to a full sitting position.

"Thanks," Becky smiled at last, faintly, and she blushed. "I mean that."

"My pleasure," Kate said dryly, taking in the flight attendant's bedraggled appearance. Her brand new blouse and skirt were soaked through, leaving very little to the imagination under the suffused glow of *la luna* – the moon. Becky's short blonde hair was plastered against her head, and water dripped down from her nose and chin. She looked like a half-drowned kitten.

Catherine Phillips began to laugh, a low, rumbling laugh, starting from deep within her belly, rising, gaining momentum, until it burst out over the dock.

"What's so funny?"

"You. You ought to see yourself."

"Oh," Becky's voice was indignant, "like you'd win any fashion awards right now, Miss 'Ninja Mutant Lifesaver'." She reached out and plucked a sodden piece of yesterday's newspaper from the pilot's shoulder.

"It's a look," Kate gamely replied. "Maybe we should go tell Maria all about this."

"Right," Becky began chuckling in spite of herself. "A new look for fall: 'Tiber'."

Kate was laughing uproariously now, gasping for breath. "Well, it looks *mahvelous* on you, *darrrrling.* "

"You too, *bella*," Becky said haughtily, before breaking up again.

Eventually their laughter died down, and they turned their attention back to the barge. The *polizia* had restored order and were mopping up, taking a few people away in handcuffs. The two American women were long forgotten by now, and on the darkened dock along the riverbank, they would have been invisible to anyone aboard.

"Oh well," Kate sighed, and she began to shiver. "Guess we'd better slink away."

"Hey." She felt a warm hand on her back. "Are you okay?"

"Fine," the pilot said through gritted teeth. "Just a little nippy after that dip." She turned slowly towards her companion, afraid of what she might see, and was shocked at the intensity of the green fire she saw in the young girl's eyes.

Kate briefly fought a battle with herself, and lost. Hell, it was one she'd never wanted to win, anyway. She reached out a hand and traced a path along Becky's arm. "You're cold, too."

"Not really," full lips opened to hers, "not now."

Thinking back on it later, Catherine couldn't be sure who had made the first move. Perhaps it was because they'd met each other halfway, or perhaps it was because it was something they'd both wanted so much, for so long, that there was no discernible beginning or end. Just the 'now' of it.

Hanson was right, she wasn't cold, Kate considered, feeling the heat of the woman's kiss, the steam rising from her flesh. That warmth flowed into the pilot, melting the chill away, fueling her strength. She deepened the kiss, her tongue finding Rebecca's own and playing with it; she deftly twisted her body over-top the smaller woman, running her hands up and down her dewy-moist skin. Her senses were screaming at her, telling her that this was everything she'd ever wanted, right here. Right now.

On a gently swaying, broken-down dock in the Tiber.

"Rebecca," Kate groaned, pulling her lips away, pausing to drink in the desire she found on Becky's face. *No.* It was all too much. Too fast. "I – I—"

"Yes?" Becky's breath came in short gasps, and she closed her eyes, placing her hands lightly behind Kate's neck. "What is it?"

"I – I'm sorry." Using every ounce of discipline she had, the pilot wrenched herself away. "I can't."

The flight attendant's green eyes snapped open. "What?"

"We've got to get out of here." Kate shakily got to her feet, firming her resolve, and hating herself for it.

"You're joking, right?"

"You shouldn't be out here like this, soaking wet." Kate turned away.

"I wasn't aware I was uncomfortable," Becky said angrily, a flush creeping across her face. She felt like a half-drowned fool. How could she have thought that this stone-faced woman before her actually gave a damn?

"Let's go." Kate's voice was flat. Dead. The pilot held out a hand to help Rebecca up, but the smaller woman ignored it.

The hurt, the rejection that Becky feared so much, had found her at last. It welled up inside her chest like bitter, choking pill.

Swallow. There's a good girl.

"Fuck you, Captain Frosty," Rebecca said savagely, slapping Kate soundly across the cheek. Squaring her shoulders, shivering, she turned her back on the pilot and walked away without another word.

Small. Vulnerable. Alone.

Catherine Phillips stood stock-still, a reddened handprint blooming on the side of her face, numbly watching her leave. She welcomed into her heart the pain that assaulted her, embracing it like an old friend.

The only friend she'd ever known

Chapter
5

Rebecca Hanson had no clear memory of how she got back to the Pensione Ausonia. Her walk was a darkened, raging blur; storming past the tightly shuttered shops of the Via Condotti, pausing once to tear off her right shoe. She could only surmise that its mate lay somewhere on the bottom of the Tiber.

Barefoot, damp, and cold, she passed blindly through the cobbled Piazza di Spagna, ignoring the frank stares of the few people gathered there for a late-night glass of wine or cappuccino. Finally, she pushed through the creaky door of the *pensione.*

Still furious, she chose the stairs, preferring to walk up the four flights rather than use the lift.

Ha! Take THAT, Catherine Phillips. Her feet slapped on the cold tiles of the lobby as she blew past Signora Canova, sitting at her usual station behind the desk.

"Miss Hanson." The older woman's *sigaretta* tumbled from her mouth into her lap, and she leaped to her feet, brushing her hands against her colorful butterfly dress. "What happen, *bella?* Where Miss Phillips?" Her pince-nez popped off the bridge of her nose and were saved from hitting the floor by the safety chain around her neck.

"Good *night,* Signora Canova," Becky said firmly, holding up a silencing hand as she marched up the steps. Granted, she'd never seen the *signora* so animated, but the last thing she wanted to do was have a conversation with her about her misadventures this evening. God, the sooner she could put all this humiliation behind her, the better.

How could she have been so stupid? So wrong?

Her breathing was labored by the time she rounded the final marble landing to the fifth floor. Maybe the steps hadn't been such a bright idea after all. She padded down the hallway and let herself into the empty, quiet room.

Becky stood there for a time in the dark, among the antique furnishings, listening to the soft noises of the square filtering through the open window. She walked over to it and, after a moment's hesitation, slammed it shut.

She wanted to block it out... all of it: the cool night air, the sounds of people enjoying themselves, any trace of Catherine Phillips.

A chill raced through her, and she headed towards the bathroom, stripping off her sodden blouse, kicking out of her skirt as she went. The soreness of her stiffened body matched the ache in her soul, and the events of the day caught up with her in a rush, taking their toll. The young flight attendant decided a bath might help with both.

She stepped onto the cool tiles, closing the door quietly behind her, and flipped on the low lights above the gilt-edged vanity mirror. A twist of a handle later, and the great, claw-footed porcelain tub began to fill with warm, steamy water.

Becky's gaze fell upon the basket of bath salts. *Why not?* she thought. She picked up a lilac-colored bottle, sniffed the flowery scent of its contents, and poured it into the water. A light layer of fragrant bubbles began to form just above the water line.

She didn't have to worry about getting her wound wet any longer, and it wasn't as if she'd had a choice earlier, anyway. So she peeled the damp gauze off her shoulder, pleased that the action hadn't hurt her too much at all. With a heavy sigh, she stepped into the tub, sat down, and eased herself cautiously against the back of it, welcoming the contrast of the cool surface against her gradually warming skin.

As bubbles continued to rise around her, Becky closed her eyes and allowed her head to droop back against the lip of the tub. Slowly, her anger seeped out from deep within her pores and released into the soothing, scented waters, taking with it the remnants of her embarrassment.

Just what the hell had happened back there? A magical day had segued into an enchanted evening, and she'd been having a fantastic time on that barge – at least until the fight had broken out. But there had been Catherine Phillips, calling out to her, showing her the way, and she knew she'd be all right. She'd used the pilot's blue eyes as her anchor as she'd maneuvered along the narrow deck, leaving the brawl behind her. She had almost made it – was reaching out to take the tall woman's hand – and then she'd found herself flying 'noggin over teacups' into the water.

She'd been disoriented for a moment until she'd fought her way back to the surface, and then she was too busy choking and sputtering out river water, to stop Kate from launching herself off the back of the barge.

By that time, Becky had found herself closer to the dock than to the floating nightspot, and so she'd stroked over to the side of it and waited there, unable to hoist herself up one-armed. The rioting on the barge had gone on unabated, and the seconds had stretched into... God – it had seemed like hours, and still the pilot had not reappeared.

Becky wasn't the strongest swimmer in the world, but she wasn't about to float idly by and do nothing. What if Kate had hit her head on that dive – or worse? And so she'd been about to release her hold on the low dock and strike out on her own rescue mission, when the still waters of the Tiber had parted, revealing Kate Phillips' dark head and broad shoulders. The overwhelming relief that had flooded through Becky then was nearly indescribable.

Later, as they'd lain side-by-side on the moonlit dock, laughing, realizing they'd both survived yet another close call, Becky's senses had been sizzling on overload. She simply couldn't get close enough to the pilot, couldn't resist any opportunity – no matter how contrived or unnecessary – to reach out and touch her bronze, silken skin.

She'd decided, then, to take a chance. It was worth it.

And when their laughter had faded away, when there was nothing but the soft glow of the moon and a zephyr of a breeze, Kate had turned to her with a look in her eyes that Becky knew had mirrored her own. Yearning. Desire. A painful, burning need that refused to be quenched unless... unless –

Becky groaned and slid down further in the nearly full tub, turning off the tap with her foot.

They had kissed.

And kissed again.

In a purely physical sense, Becky had been rocked by her body's response to Kate's caresses. It was as though a blast of high-volt-age electricity had jolted through her body. Still, it wasn't enough. She wanted more. Much more. And to her delight, it seemed Kate had felt the same. She would've sworn to it. There was no way she'd been mistaken – no way. Not when she thought back to how the pilot had reacted to the contact – how her skin had thrummed in response to Becky's own touch.

Yes, Rebecca Hanson, for once in her life, was willing to risk it all. To surrender her heart and body to this woman who'd occupied her every waking and dreaming thought since the moment she'd first met her.

Now.

She was ready.

To her boundless, searing humiliation, Captain Catherine Phillips, evidently, was not.

Intermittent drops from the faucet plunked into the tub. The water slowly lapped against the porcelain sides at her every subtle movement, with every gentle breath. The heat of the bath was working, relaxing her muscles and taking away the coldness of her plunge into the river. Becky closed her eyes once more, and thought about the look on Kate's face when she had slapped her. God, what had come over her? She'd never done anything like that before in her whole life. It was just that... the hurt inside – it was too much. And so she'd snapped.

She could feel the rejection all over again now. It was a dull pang blossoming in her chest, a tightness gripping her there. This time, instead of striking out, Becky simply lifted a trembling hand to her head, and began to cry.

When Catherine Phillips trailed through the lobby just a few moments after Rebecca Hanson, a worried Signora Canova had barely re-settled behind her desk, still reeling from Becky's fly-by. Why, that poor little child. After all she'd been through – the *signora* had read those stories in the newspapers – what had happened this night to give her such an appearance? No wonder the girl had seemed so distraught.

Now, here came her friend, that pilot: tall, dark – and drenched, just like Miss Hanson had been. The American woman squished her way across the lobby, and Signora Canova opened her mouth as if to speak. This was her *pensione,* and she had a right to know what was going on. She'd always thought that big one was trouble from the first moment her shadow had crossed the door of the Ausonia.

But no words came, for the *signora* found herself impaled on two piercing, threatening blue eyes. *Dio...* The air whooshed from her lungs as though she'd been hit.

A fiery storm raged within that Catherine Phillips; she could see it now, a swirling deadly power behind that icy gaze. The *signora* prudently determined that she'd do well to find safe harbor elsewhere.

Not wanting to give in entirely, she sniffed down her pince-nez at the younger woman, nervously fingering her bun, and then turned to retrieve some paperwork from the small office behind her desk. It needed to be done anyway, she rationalized, and now was as good a time as any. With a brusque nod, she watched the sullen pilot pass. Like her friend before her, she chose the stairs.

Signora Canova knew a *diavolo* – 'devil' – when she saw one. The sooner the beast was gone, the better.

Catherine Phillips was numb.

It had nothing to do with the clamminess of her skin, thanks to the river-damp clothes that clung to her. Nor was it associated with the cooling breezes of the Roman nighttime that had been biting at her heels every step of the chilly walk back.

Rather, it was a numbness she compared to what death must be like, she thought, as she trudged up the worn marble steps of the *pensione* to the fifth floor. She couldn't feel, couldn't think, was closed off to anything and anyone around her, content to exist only in this exquisitely painful prison that she alone had constructed.

Where she alone had chosen to live, without regard to what others might think. Or what others might wish for her.

In that state of emotionless isolation, she hadn't known what else to do, but to return to the *pensione.* Even if she'd wanted to bolt for the airport immediately and hitch a ride somewhere... *anywhere,* she was a pilot – first and foremost. And pilots never left their flight kits behind. She fully intended to retrieve her case full of charts, navigational tools, and reports, and then get the hell out of the Pensione Ausonia.

And Rebecca Hanson's life.

Before she did any more damage.

As if tonight hadn't been bad enough, when she allowed her raging desires to trample the good common sense she'd been born with. Her life was in a power-dive to nowhere, and there was no way she planned on letting the sweet, beautiful young Rebecca Hanson crash and burn along with her.

She'd just grab her kit and go. That was all there was to it.

Kate eased open the paneled door to room number two, and was surprised to find it dark.

Empty.

And warm.

Instinctively, the pilot walked to the window and flung it open. A light breeze immediately pushed its way in, billowing the curtains, cooling the room.

Kate glanced around the murky interior, but her battered soul took comfort in the dark, and so she opted not to turn on a light. Where was Hanson? Perhaps she hadn't even made it back to the *pensione?* A flutter of worry tugged at the pilot's gut, thinking of Hanson catching pneumonia on the streets of Rome, but with some effort she managed to shove that thought aside. This way, at least, she could get what she needed and leave without another awkward encounter.

The tall woman was taking a step towards the walk-in closet, when she stumbled on something soft. In the dark, she couldn't tell exactly what it was. She reached down, and plucked up a beige beaded, and decidedly soggy – skirt.

Hanson, it appeared, had already arrived.

It was then that Catherine noticed a faint light creeping out from under the bathroom door. And then, too, when her ears pricked at the unmistakable sound of Hanson crying. Good God – how many times was this, now? As quickly as the irritation flared in Kate, it withered and died; the pilot knew well enough that this was the first time the girl had been driven to tears because of her.

So.

She'd succeeded in doing the one thing she'd sworn to herself that she would never do: hurt Rebecca Hanson.

Kate moved to just outside the bathroom, and lightly tapped on the door.

"Hanson?"

"Go away," a muffled voice retorted.

"Hanson, please, don't cry."

"Leave – me – alone." And with that, Becky's weeping intensified.

Damn. "Hanson. Rebecca... please." She pressed on the door and it opened slightly. "I – I'm sorry. I didn't mean to hurt you. I— " A frustrated sigh. "I... would never..."

"A little late for that now, isn't it?" Becky's voice was clearer, harder, through the partially opened door. "Although I don't know why it even matters to you at all. It's obvious you want *nothing* to do with me."

"No Rebecca, that's not it," Catherine groaned. She leaned against the doorframe, squeezing her eyes shut. The door itself edged open a bit more, and the pilot could hear the water in the tub slapping against the sides with Becky's agitated movements. "I do care for you. Maybe *too* much." She lowered her head in the dark. "I'm no good for you."

"Since when do you decide what's good for me and what's not?" It was obvious Becky was struggling to regain some sort of control, to stem the flow of her tears.

"No, Rebecca," Kate said quietly, "you deserve better than me. Someone who will," she gritted her teeth, "love... you, the way you... deserve to be loved. The way you've always dreamed it could be."

A bitter laugh echoed off the tiles. "Funny. I've never felt worse in my life than I do right now, because the person I've dreamed of, waited for – she... is right here in front of me. And you don't give a damn."

"Rebecca... no." Kate couldn't help it. She pushed the door open the rest of the way. There was Hanson, sitting in the great tub, looking so very small. She held her knees up tightly to her chest, and pieces of her short hair hung limp and damp in the hazy steam of the bubble bath. Twin tear-tracks streaked down her beautiful face. Dammit, what was the matter with her? Didn't the girl realize that Catherine Phillips was a sucker's bet? "No." She shook her head, "You'll see... later... that this is all for the best."

Sad, reddened eyes swung up to the pilot and glistened in the soft light. "You're wrong. It's you, Kate," Becky insisted. "Even though I have no idea half the time what the hell I'm talking about... thinking about... God help me, it's you."

The dark woman walked onto the tile floor, and knelt next to the tub. She rested an arm along the rim. "Ah, Hanson, you don't know what you're saying."

"I'm telling you how I *feel*, Kate," she said in a trembling voice. "You ought to try it, sometime."

The pilot whipped her head away as though she'd been struck.

It was true. Who had more to lose here, anyway? Hanson was laying everything on the line, as simply and honestly, as she knew how. So typical of her. And all she, Catherine could do was spout her usual bullshit of how it could never work, about how it wasn't right that they get involved – when the pounding in her chest told her Rebecca Hanson was the one thing she desired more than life itself.

So, what *was* holding her back? What was her fucking problem?

Christ, maybe she should just open her own goddamned eyes and learn something for once. From Hanson.

Deep breath. "I'm scared," she said softly. There. It was out.

"Oh, Kate... What—"

"I'm fucking scared, okay?" The pilot's voice was a shout. Kate closed her eyes against the pain of it all, and rested her head in her hand, determined not to stop until she'd put it all out there, as Hanson had. "I'm not sure I even know *how* to love somebody," she croaked, a tear slipping from the corner of a closed eyelid. "Not... not when I hate myself so much."

Kate took in a hitching, heaving gulp of air, sucking it deep into her gut, as she struggled to maintain her composure. Dammit. With Hanson, nothing was ever easy.

There was silence, then. Nothing, save for the gentle lapping of the water against the sides of the tub.

The movement of it increased slightly, and then Kate felt a warm, wet hand hesitantly make contact with her cheek.

Oh, shit. A surge of desire raced through her like a wildfire, out of control, uncaring what destruction was left in its wake. Rebecca Hanson was hurting. Kate could tell that much, and she was the cause of it. She'd do anything to take that pain away. And it was obvious right now that Hanson needed to be held.

To be shown some affection.

Hell, if it was just about sex, Catherine Phillips could get the job done. And maybe feel a little bit better about herself in the process. All that other bullshit... love... well, she could worry about it later.

Eyes still closed, she turned towards the dripping hand, nuzzling it.

"Kate..."

The hand opened, dropping to cup her chin, and Kate's breathing quickened. *No, no, no!*

Her mind screamed, even as she grabbed the hand with her own, and licked its opened palm... kissed it.

She heard a tremulous sigh release from Rebecca Hanson.

And that was all the permission Catherine Phillips needed, to gladly shred away her last, lingering shield of self-discipline.

She swiveled around and lunged at Becky, sweeping her up and half out of the tub. She heard the younger woman gasp in shock as she ravenously began to devour her like the dangerous, wild animal she was; hands raking through her hair, lips finding every available square inch of moist, scented skin; tongue pressing and plunging into a sweet, welcoming mouth.

In one swift, smooth motion, Kate vaulted into the oversized tub, oblivious to the water sloshing over the sides. It streamed down past the clawed feet and across the floor like a miniature tidal surge; but Kate was uncaring of the second soaking her clothes were taking this night. She lowered Becky back down into the warm, bubbly waters, pressing her attack.

There was no hope now of restraining her cravings, no thought of engaging in a lingering, easy flirtation with the promise of a passion to come. Kate's nerve endings were on overdrive, and she could tell by Becky's breathless, hot-blooded response, by the wet hands running though her damp hair and digging into her back, that she felt the same way.

Kate kept her eyes closed for a time, unwilling to look at Becky, fearful of opening herself up to whatever rawness of feeling and honesty of emotion she might find upon the younger woman's face, or see, reflected in her eyes.

But finally, Kate could stand it no longer. She paused, drawing in air with heaving spurts. Blue eyes opened to green, and the pilot nearly lost herself in the slow-burning heat she discovered there. Becky's lips were a bruised cherry-red, swollen and half-parted, yearning for more. Her normally pale features were flushed from the temperature of the water... scorched by the fire that burned within her. Kate allowed her eyes to drop down, to travel along a swanlike, delectable neck, falling farther still to where two firm, shapely breasts peeked their way between the softly hissing bubbles.

"You're beautiful," Kate heard herself saying.

And then there was Rebecca's own voice. Hoarse. Needful. "Love me."

With a spurred-on sense of urgency, the pilot renewed her assault. She angled herself sideways next to Becky, and her own breathing caught when she felt two small hands tugging at the sides of the sleeveless white blouse plastered to her body. Kate shifted so that the top came off, easily sliding over her head.

She never heard the *fop* of it hitting the soaked, tiled floor, so distracted was she by the burning touch of Becky's hands upon the nakedness of her skin. A hot chill skipped through her, and she eagerly turned her attention to the flight attendant's left breast, teasing the nipple with her slow, circling tongue. Eyes half closed, lost in the sensation, she leaned her left arm around Hanson and supported herself against the back of the tub, using her free hand to knead the responsive, rounded flesh on the woman's right side.

Kate let her fingertips trace downwards, feathering over a tautly muscled abdomen, and she delighted in Rebecca's gasp as her hand fell lower still, plunging beneath the roiling water, finding and seizing her hot center.

Weakly, Becky grasped for the waistband of Kate's blue capri pants. "No," a dark head lifted, and she moved the girl's hand away, pressing it against her wildly pumping heart, "let me..." and she covered Becky's mouth with her own, kissing, licking, biting, even as her hand began to awaken the smaller woman with a gentle, probing rhythm. Quickly, the motion became more forced in tempo, stroking, pressing, and Rebecca arched her back into it... ground her hips... crying out at the exquisite torture of the pilot's ministrations.

Catherine could feel the pressure building in the core of her young lover, and the cloth of her pants against the bottom of the tub gave her the leverage she needed to help guide Becky home. She gave no thought to her own satisfaction; her joy was in seeing the glazed look of desire on the young blonde's face, in hearing the ragged pulls of her breath as she took her pleasure.

"Oh... God... Kate!" Becky's voice was strangled now, and her arms circled tightly around the taller woman's neck.

Kate's pulse throbbed in her veins, churning, set off merely by the simple sound of Rebecca calling her name.

Their coupling was frantic. Reckless. Water continued to spray up from the bath; the pilot was completely soaked. Kate tilted her head up and locked her eyes on Becky's now, accelerating her fingered thrusts. Soon, the soft whimpers in the back of the girl's throat grew into choking moans; with one final plunge, the sound exploded into a primal cry of release. Kate immediately silenced it with a heated, searing kiss, pouring all of her heart, her hopes, her dreams, into the vessel that was Rebecca Hanson.

They lay there for a time, each unwilling to break contact, and Kate worked her way around so that she half supported Becky from behind. With a casual possessiveness, she allowed her hands to slowly stroke Rebecca's arms, her face, her stomach, relishing her nearness.

Gradually, the bubbles broke, the waters cooled, and their breathing began to settle and slow. Kate dipped her head down and placed a lazy kiss on the top of Becky's wet, golden hair, and the young woman slowly turned her face up to her, and smiled. *God...* For a moment, Kate's heart skipped a beat at the simple beauty of her. At the honesty of emotion, of adoration on her face. *Dammit,* the pilot thought, *she almost makes me feel like the woman I wish I could be.*

Impulsively, Becky strained upwards to kiss away a droplet of water from the tip of the pilot's nose. "Kate," she sighed, reaching a hand around her waist, "I want t–to—" But a shudder coursed through her, thanks to the water's chill.

"No... ssshhh. You just relax." Displaying very little effort, Kate swept an arm under the flight attendant's knees and swung another around her back. She easily lifted her from the tub and lightly deposited her on the slippery floor. "Careful." Kate reached for a large, thirsty white towel, and wrapped a shivering Rebecca Hanson in it as though she were a child. A drowsy grin on the young girl's rosy-fresh features turned into a barely stifled yawn.

"What are you doing?" Becky lifted a tired eyebrow at her.

"Bedtime for you, Hanson." With a faint smile, Kate grabbed another towel for herself and, against Becky's giggling protests, picked her up again and carried her out to the four-poster bed. Carefully, gently, she laid her down beneath the flowered canopy. Kate quickly shrugged off her own soaked pants, draped the towel around her long form, and climbed into bed next to Hanson.

Becky yawned again. "Mm-hmm... so tired..."

Before Kate even had a chance to pull the fluffy comforter up around them, Becky squirmed close to the airline pilot, casually throwing an arm across her stomach, nudging her head into the crook of the taller woman's shoulder.

"'G'night, Kate," she murmured as her eyes fluttered and closed. In the moon glow, Kate could see that a satisfied smile still lingered on her delicate face.

"Sleep well," the pilot said softly, and she already knew by the flight attendant's deep, even breathing, that she hadn't heard. Kate couldn't help it, she lowered her head and lightly kissed each of Becky's closed eyelids, let her fingers carefully skip over the healing, stitched area of her shoulder, until at last she simply lay there, watching the steady rise and fall of Rebecca's chest.

God, how this sweet, loving woman had given herself up to her this night, without a moment's hesitation, without recrimination, without judgment. And Catherine Phillips had welcomed every blessed bit of it, and come surging back for more. She let her thoughts idly shift towards what a life with Rebecca Hanson might have been like, and allowed herself to revel, for a time, in that fleeting moment of joy. To catch a tantalizing glimpse of a happiness she would never know.

For who did she think she was kidding? She didn't deserve the likes of Rebecca. Sure, she'd taken away the young woman's pain, at least for tonight. But in the long run, Hanson would see she'd been right... that she'd be better off, *much* better off, without her. The flight attendant might be hurt, for a while, but tall, blonde 'somebodies' like Alan Ross, would be only too eager to help her heal, she was sure of it.

Kate softly nuzzled Becky's damp hair, breathing in deeply of the light, flowered scent. It would have to do her for a lifetime, she sadly thought. Cautiously, she disentangled herself from the exhausted woman, and Becky did not stir, so soundly did she sleep.

The pilot moved like a silent ghost about the room, dressing in her Orbis Airlines uniform, pulling back her drying hair in a clip, packing her things. She knew Orbis had an early-morning flight out of Fiumicino, back to New York, and she was determined to be on it.

Finished.

Kate's hand was on the ancient, brass doorknob, when she hesitated. She carefully lowered her flight kit and bag to the floor, and then walked over to the writing desk near the window. There, by the light of the moon and the morning stars, she scribbled a few lines to Hanson.

She was doing the right thing; she knew it. So why did it feel as if an invisible monster were squeezing the very life out of her chest? Why did her stomach feel as though she had a fist twisting in it, ripping at her guts? God, how her pulse was racing. If she closed her eyes, she could still feel the hot breath of Rebecca Hanson against her face, begging, pleading for more…

No. Hanson didn't deserve such damaged goods. Time to run away. Again.

Guiltily, selfishly, Kate paused by the side of the bed, and studied Hanson for a moment. This woman who might've been her future, if only she'd had the guts. This woman who, though she'd only known her for a few days, felt as familiar to her as the sum of her own existence. Kate pressed two fingers to her lips, and then reached down and touched them to Hanson's. In her sleep, the young woman lightly puckered at the contact, and then resumed her peaceful repose.

Let her dream.

Kate gulped, hard, and tore herself away.

Ah well, she sighed, picking up her bags and reaching a shaking hand for the doorknob. *Fuck. Fuck me.* She dared not look back at Hanson now, or else she might never leave.

A creaking click of the door, a sliver of light, and she was gone.

It took a lot of training, not to feel. It took concentration, commitment, and practice to make one's self utterly immune to caring, and Catherine Phillips had been toiling away at it for years.

And just when the pilot thought she'd had it down cold, Rebecca Hanson had blown into her life like a summer squall, catching her by surprise, leaving her exposed to forces of nature she'd had no intention of ever dealing with again.

Affection.

Desire.

Love.

Some part of Catherine had actually flirted for a time with the thought that there just might be something to it. For there were moments when she'd gazed upon Hanson, when the smaller woman wasn't looking, and found herself viewing the world through her eyes. Eyes eager, wide-open and without guile. And Kate had half-considered, then, that any and all things were possible in the face of such innocence.

But no... a cold blast of a wind shear had slammed her back down to earth, rudely awakened her, shattered her blue-sky dreaming.

Don't feel. Don't care. Don't *think.* That was her mantra during the taxi ride all the way back to Fiumicino. Dawn was just breaking when she'd stormed through the empty lobby of the *pensione;* even the ubiquitous Signora Canova had to sleep sometime. Kate hadn't bothered to ring a cab from the lobby, knowing there was a taxi stand at the edge of the Piazza di Spagna. She just wanted to get the hell *out* of the building before anyone was the wiser.

Shit, she thought, *I'm a grown woman! So why do I feel like I'm running away from home?*

Sure enough, even at that early hour, a lone Fiat Punta sat at the stand. As Kate had approached, the lights winked on, cutting through the foggy air, and the engine growled to life.

"Fiumicino," Kate had barked, throwing her kit and bag into the back seat with her. She'd noticed immediately that the cab was meterless. He was probably a gypsy driver, taking advantage of the off-hours fares. When she had asked him the cost to the airport, he'd quoted her 120,000 Lire – an outrageous sum. But he could've quoted triple that number, and the pilot would not have complained. The end justified the means.

Although... A slow smile crept onto her face as she considered how Hanson would've been scandalized at the price, and haggled the driver down or to his death, whichever came first. But Hanson wasn't here.

Kate was alone.

In silence, they had driven on the expressway out of the city, racing away from the rising sun, leaving Rome, and Hanson, behind. As jumbled buildings gave way to open space and umbrella pines, it had seemed to Kate that the last few days of her holiday were simply rewinding – as though they had never happened. In time, maybe she'd come to believe it herself. *Don't feel. Don't think.*

Kate ignored the surprised looks thrown her way when she checked in at Fiumicino's Orbis lounge. Stories of the hijacking were still hot news for the flight attendants, agents, and pilots scattered about the facility.

No matter. She wasn't interested in discussing any of it.

And so, after flashing her I.D. and volunteering as a 'fly along' alternate on the 7:05 a.m. departure to JFK, she grabbed a newspaper and espresso, and settled down in a far-away corner of the lounge.

"H – hi, Captain… Phillips, is it? How are you?"

A pair of icy blue eyes lifted up from behind the newspaper, to take in a young sandy-haired steward. He looked vaguely familiar, and Kate imagined she must've served with him somewhere along the line in her Orbis travels.

"Hi." Her voice was flat. Uninterested.

"Wow," he laughed excitedly, holding out his hand, "I thought it was you. I'm Josh. Josh Peters."

Kate ignored the outstretched hand. Maybe if she ignored him, the kid would go way.

He stuffed the hand into his pocket, as though he didn't quite know to whom it belonged. Still, he pressed ahead, his morbid curiosity outweighing his fear. "Man, I read all about that hijacking. You and Becky Hanson and—"

"Look, *Josh,*" Kate's eyes glittered and narrowed, "I *do* want to read my newspaper, I *don't* want to talk about the hijacking and, most of all, I *don't* want to talk to you. *Capisce?*"

Josh Peters blushed deeply, down to the roots of his fair hair. His mouth bobbed open once or twice like a fish out of water, before he finally mumbled a "Sorry, lady," and turned on his heels, stalking away.

Captain Frosty the Snow Bitch, they all called her – even Hanson. She knew that. She knew why. Fuck 'em. She didn't care. *Don't think. Don't feel.*

Catherine took another sip of the black, bitter espresso, idly considering how it matched her mood, and she let her eyes run across the lines of the newspaper, not reading a goddamned word of it.

It was just a dream… it had to be. The same one she'd been having for days, now. So why couldn't she wake herself up? It was so dark, so cold, and just where the heck was she anyway? She was so lost… so far away from home. How would she ever make it back?

The darkness grew deeper, the cold, more numbing, and she was scared now, really scared. She wanted to run, but she didn't know in which direction to go. And she was frozen now, anyway. Unable to move. Unable to think clearly.

With a convulsed start, Rebecca Hanson realized she was awake. She could feel the flutter of her heart in her chest, even as her breath hitched in shallow gasps. *Damn, that was some dream.* she thought, rubbing her hands on her arms. Yes, she was awake. But still cold, and still alone.

Definitely alone.

A deep shudder rolled through her body. "Kate?" The silence that greeted her told her the answer she already knew. Feared.

Pushing the blankets aside, she wrapped a slightly damp towel about her as she eased out of bed and padded over to the bathroom. The door was open, and in the low lights from the vanity, Becky could see shimmering puddles of water drying on the floor.

She smiled. So, it hadn't been a dream. That, and the fading, pleasant ache she felt in her nether regions, confirmed it.

Now, where the heck was Catherine Phillips?

The young blonde traded her damp towel for a fresh one, and stepped out into the main room. God, it was cold.

"Kate," she called out again, feeling slightly silly as she did so. It was obvious the pilot wasn't there. She sighed, and walked over to the open window. A cool breeze pushed through the curtains, and Becky coughed, drawing the window closed. She paused, looking out over the *piazza.*

The cobbled stones were still dark-wet from an early morning mist that had nearly lifted. Atop the Spanish Steps, the promise of the morning sun was beginning to bloom and glow from behind the twin spires of the Franciscan Church of *Trinità dei Monti.* Birdsong filled the air, though Becky couldn't even see the little creatures yet, still huddled as they were in their nests.

A small tan and white terrier trotted across the square, unescorted, snuffling at the doorways and lampposts along its way. Entranced, Becky watched the animal until it rounded a corner and disappeared. Only then did she allow her eyes to drop to the writing desk next to her.

To see the ivory parchment paper lying mutely on the tabletop, with the few lines of a strong, firm script flowing across the center of it.

Becky felt her body begin to tremble uncontrollably. She had to force her eyes to read the words she found there, just visible in the dim light of dawn.

Rebecca –

You saved my life, in more ways than one.
I can't take away yours.
Forget about me, and live!

Sincerely,
Catherine

No. It couldn't be. A single tear fell upon the page, smearing Catherine's signature. This was a nightmare, all right, Becky thought, lifting her eyes from the damnable letter to the empty, tumbled poster bed.

If only she were dreaming.

Catherine Phillips ignored the dull pounding that started at the base of her skull. It crept halfway up the back of her head, before it plunged through the middle of her brain, stabbing at the back of her eyes. Aspirin. She knew right where they were in Hanson's backpack. That kid was prepared for anything, she thought, remembering the collapsible little umbrella, the Band-aids, the sunscreen. In any event, the pilot wished she had a few of those little white tablets right now.

No matter. She'd be on Orbis Flight 360 to New York soon enough. Certainly, she'd be able to grab a few painkillers on board. Typically, the 7:05 a.m. departure was never a full flight and, even with the strike, Kate doubted it would be now. Perfect. She planned on sleeping her way back to the states. Escaping in her dreams. She was good at that.

Looking tall and trim in her indigo Orbis slacks and blazer, white blouse, and overcoat, Kate moved swiftly along the international concourse, nodding a greeting to the people at the security checkpoint. It was still some distance to gate 20 where an Orbis Boeing 757 was preparing for take-off, but Kate's long legs carried her quickly through the walkway. She'd been given an open first class seat, no doubt in deference to her so-called heroics earlier in the week, and she intended on waiting until the last minute to board the big jet. She preferred the open air of the terminal to the restricted spaces of the passenger cabin. The pilot always felt out of sorts anyway when she was on a plane she wasn't captaining… losing just that little bit of control.

Kate arrived at the gate just as a herd of passengers were being shepherded towards the jetway by half-awake flight agents. Taking tickets, checking the sizes of carry-ons, calling out rows; the pilot had seen and heard it all countless times. Sounds of the crowd were fairly subdued; many passengers were exhausted returning vacationers, business people, school kids. Everyone with a face, everyone with a name, just like those aboard Flight 2240, her plane that had almost fallen into the sea. Kate would never take these routine actions – these living, breathing souls – for granted again.

The pilot moved over to a large, tinted window, separating herself from the people gathered at the gate. There, in the far corner, it was quieter. And more secluded. Also, it gave her the best angle to look out at the plane. Painted in bold swaths of blue and gold, the signature colors of the Orbis fleet, the aircraft was a newer model, Kate could tell. Through the cabin windows, she could see passengers milling about, taking their seats. She shifted her eyes to the tarmac. There wasn't a lot of activity at this time of day; only the green, orange, and white markings of an Alitalia Airbus A-321 at a gate a few slots down. Just in from abroad, Kate surmised.

In the distance, Kate could see the big runway she'd landed on just a few days earlier. It stretched down the opposite side of the airport, near a grassy wetland whose sheaves of reeds rolled and rippled under the caress of a light, western breeze. The air was bright and clear, with ocean-blue skies overhead, and the chill of the early morning was beginning to dissipate. It would be a lovely day in Italy. A day she would leave far behind, although, as she squinted out the window, she could not help but wonder how Hanson would spend it.

Sure, she was bound to be upset at first when she found the note. But, Kate knew it was the only way of sparing the young blonde the pain of her having to do it later... after she'd realized the terrible mistake she'd made. And Rebecca Hanson was such a kind-hearted soul, she might not be willing to walk away and leave Kate, out of some misguided sense of... pity. There was no way the pilot could endure that. No way.

"Ladies and gentlemen, may I have your attention, please? This is the final boarding call for Orbis Flight #360, flying non-stop from Rome to New York, now boarding at gate 20. Signore e signori, posso avere vostra attenzione, prego..."

Catherine sighed heavily, and reached down to pick up her bags.

"'Sincerely'?"

A voice, raw and ragged, and as familiar to her as her own. The pilot slowly straightened and turned around, but not before catching a flash of golden hair reflected in the tinted window.

Kate gulped, hard. "Rebecca."

"'Sincerely'?" she repeated, shaking her head in disbelief. She crumpled Kate's note in her small fist and then dropped it to the floor. Both women silently watched it fall.

The young flight attendant looked terrible. Her face was puffy, and she looked as though she'd been crying. Her feathered hair was sticking out at odd angles from her head, and she wore an oversized, wrinkled Bugs Bunny t-shirt and jeans, beneath a dark-blue, regulation Orbis trench coat. Kate wasn't sure, but at first glance it looked as though the young woman's shoes didn't match.

"Kate." Becky took a faltering step closer. "Don't. Don't do this."

A dark head turned away. "Not here, Hanson."

"If not here, where? When?" Becky's voice turned demanding. Insistent. She was fighting for her life here, with this infuriating, impossible pilot, and she knew it. "When *you* decide it's okay? Just when will that be? Next week? Next month?" A choking pause. "Never?"

Kate closed her eyes against the truth of Rebecca's words. Dammit, because of this woman, she felt the worst she ever had in her entire life.

And the best.

Rebecca had openly, honestly offered herself to her... loved her. She had awakened from deep within the pilot the capacity to think... to feel emotions she'd thought were long since dead, and it scared the hell out of her.

She struggled to maintain her balance, to rein in her galloping heart, even as she breathed in the sweet, flowery scent of the smaller woman standing so close to her now. She swung her gaze back to Becky. *Flaps up.* "I have to go," she said tersely.

"This is the last call for Orbis Flight #360…"

Kate reached for her bags.

"NO!" Becky cried out, physically putting herself between the pilot and her luggage.

"Get out of my way, Hanson." Kate's voice was hard. Dammit, why wouldn't the girl just leave it alone?

"I won't." Becky grabbed the pilot's arm. "I – I love you, Kate." Her voice was desperate, pleading. And now the tears began to fall, streaming down her face. "Tell me you don't feel the same way."

The pilot stiffened, and glared at her. "I don't." Unsuccessfully, she tried to free herself of Becky's hand.

"You're lying." Becky's green eyes flashed. "After last night—"

"Last night meant nothing," Kate said coldly, steeling her heart. "I felt sorry for you, that's all."

"No!" Hurt beyond all reason, the air burst from Becky in a stunned gasp. "No…" she said weakly, dropping her arm to her side, "you don't mean that."

Kate slung her travel bag over her shoulder. "Get over yourself, Hanson," she said brusquely, tearing her own soul apart. She was almost there. She'd almost gotten Rebecca to hate her, like all the rest. It was for her own good, after all. "Do you think you're the only cute little flight attendant I've ever fucked?"

Here we go again, Kate thought. She could see the slap coming from a mile away, but she did nothing to stop it.

She felt the impact of Becky's hand on her face, and dammit, it was the same side she'd nailed her on earlier; the same side, too, that hijacker had gotten a few days before. Her tonsils rattled in the back of her throat. She heard the *smack* echo through the terminal, saw faces swing towards them and then quickly turn away. She had a headache now, all right.

"You are *some* bitch." Becky's voice shook as she wiped at her tears with the sleeve of her coat.

"Yeah, that's right," Kate said bitterly. "That's me."

"Captain Phillips, we need to seal the jetway."

Kate turned to a rather embarrassed-looking Orbis agent, standing at the doorway with a member of the ground crew.

"Coming."

The pilot turned back to Rebecca Hanson one last time, and that was her undoing. Because

Becky chose that moment to push past her own shock and hurt, and look up into the fathomless blue eyes of the noble, complex woman who stood before her.

So damned imposing, so closed off... and Becky saw the flickering emotions upon the golden, sculpted features that the pilot so desperately tried to hide. Fear. A raw, inner pain that refused to heal. And defiance, too, in the face of it all. The sum of it reached out, across the chasm, and tugged at the younger woman's heart.

And in an otherworldly burst of clarity, Becky at last understood. Dammit, this was one decision she was making for herself. She was not going to let Catherine Phillips get away.

"Okay, go ahead," Becky said with as much calmness as she could muster, stepping aside.

"Thanks," Kate grumbled, mollified. She reached for her flight kit and began to walk towards the gate.

"After all," the young blonde continued, "I can understand why you have to run out. Being so scared... and all."

"What?" Kate stopped. Blue, stony eyes turned to lock on warm green.

"You're scared." There was a triumphant gleam on Becky's face, "Scared of loving someone. Scared of *letting* yourself be loved. You said it yourself."

"You're crazy." Kate worked her jaw, frowning.

"Captain Phillips, please…" the Orbis agent pleaded.

"Go on, shoo." Becky flicked her hands at the pilot, waving her towards the gate. "You big, bad, scaredy-cat. Run away!" She stuck her tongue firmly in her cheek, as though it mattered not at all whether the pilot stayed or left.

Dammit, now why did Hanson have to put it that way? Kate thought. As if it were a challenge. A battle to be fought and won.

Catherine Phillips never backed down from a fight.

"You're wrong," Kate growled, her face darkening, clenching her fists. She took a step back towards the disheveled flight attendant.

"I am not." Becky crossed her arms in front of her chest.

"You – are – wrong." Kate's voice was a low, threatening, rumble.

But Rebecca Hanson wasn't scared. Not by a long shot. "Prove it."

In the blink of an eye, the pilot covered the remaining distance between herself and Hanson. She stood as close to her as she possibly could, and Becky could feel Kate's hot, shallow breath on her face as the tall woman's stare bored into her. Slowly, deliberately, the pilot reached for Hanson's right hand, brought it to her lips, and lightly kissed its open palm.

Becky rocked back on her heels at the electric sensation of it, sparking through her, drilling down to her toes. *God, was that a flicker of a tongue there, too?*

At last, Kate drew away, examining Becky's hand curiously. "Did anyone ever tell you that you have a mean right hook?" she smiled a little.

"Look," Becky swallowed, reeling at this sudden turn of events, "I am not a morning person, see? And there's a cabby waiting for me outside this terminal who – I think – is charging me my life savings in lire."

"Well, that doesn't sound too good," Kate said, raising an eyebrow in mock deliberation.

"And – and I wake up this morning," the words tumbled out in a rush, "to find that someone who I didn't even know I'd been waiting for all my life, intends to leave me." She boldly put her arms around Kate's waist. "Just when I'd found her."

"She must've panicked," Kate said thoughtfully, pulling Rebecca closer.

"Don't leave me, Kate. You deserve to be loved. We both… deserve it." Becky searched the pilot's face for the answer she needed to see. "Give us that chance." A lone tear slipped out of the corner of her eye, and the pilot thumbed it away.

"Ah… Rebecca…" Dammit, there Hanson was, crying again.

Well, there would be no more tears for the girl, Kate would see to that. What the hell, the young woman *did* have a point. It seemed that her whole life had been spent running, search-ing. Desperately looking for answers, for mean-ing.

Maybe, just maybe, in Rebecca Hanson, she'd found them.

"Kate, please," Becky cried, burying her head in the taller woman's chest.

Nope. No more tears. None of that bullshit. Kate decided to stop them the only way she knew how.

A fingertip lifting a quivering chin, a dark head dipping low, and lips meeting in a soft, gentle kiss.

Kate held the younger woman close, relish-ing the nearness of her, the rightness of it all. "Ssssh..." She moved her lips to the side and whispered in Becky's ear, "Don't cry."

"Captain..." The Orbis agent was desperate now. Torn between facing the wrath of the pilot on the plane or the fury of the notorious pilot at the gate. "I must insist."

Kate finally pulled away, and let an easy grin over-spread her face. She looked down at Hanson's bloodshot eyes, her puffy face, and her mismatched shoes.

God, she is beautiful.

With a quick, reassuring squeeze of Becky's arms, the pilot turned towards the anxious Orbis agent.

"Ahem." As she cleared her throat, she could do nothing to prevent a slow, crimson blush from rising to her cheeks, "You can seal the jetway." She swung her gaze back to Rebecca. "I'm staying."

Chapter
6

The daily bustle of the Piazza di Spagna was building nicely, as the morning sunlight streamed onto the square like burnished ribbons of gold: rich, warm, intoxicating. Shopkeepers clicked open heavy doors and threw open their window shutters, readying for a new day of business. Many Romans used the *piazza* as a shortcut to the Via Sistini or the Via Crispi, and so there were suited office workers, men and women alike, wearing sunglasses and disinterested expressions. They hurried without seeming to hurry, in that languid ease which is uniquely Italian.

In contrast, schoolchildren paused to stop at the fountain, the boys in dark pants, ties, and white shirts, proving their bravery in the face of splashes from the maroon-skirted girls who pretended not to notice them at all.

Rebecca Hanson sat on the balcony outside her room at the *pensione,* taking it all in, savoring it, and found herself amazed at how her life had completely changed its heading in less than a week. Been turned upside down, as a matter of fact.

Just work a one-off flight to Rome, she'd thought, take in a few days sightseeing, and then fly back to New York. Or wherever else Orbis Airlines deigned fit to send her.

A terrorist hijacking, getting shot, falling in love – none of these heart-stopping events were in her plans. Most unusual, for a woman who liked to plan and organize... see to every last detail. Her rather extensive sightseeing agenda of Rome was proof enough of that.

Looking out over the wrought iron balcony rail, Becky yawned and smiled at the memory of how Catherine Phillips had put her itinerary in the shredder. Loudly dismissed her ambitious plans out-of-hand. And then promptly shown her the most breathtaking few days of her entire life, capturing Becky's heart in the process.

Most unexpected.

Heck, she thought, *it was the last freaking thing I thought would ever happen to me.*

Falling so hard, so fast, and for another woman, no less. Not according to plan. But the tall, dark airline pilot stirred something in Becky that she'd never felt before, not even close. If she was truly honest with herself, she would admit that she'd felt the initial flutterings of it the moment she'd first caught sight of Kate across the crowded terminal at JFK.

And God, after last night… there was no way she could ever give that up. Not willingly. Not ever.

When that nightmare had awakened her and she'd found herself alone with that blasted note, at first she'd been paralyzed with shock. But then, quickly, her instincts had taken over and she'd forced herself to think, to plan.

She knew there was only one place the runaway pilot would've headed.

The airport.

Somehow, some way, she'd reached deep down inside herself and found the guts to scramble into some clothes and follow her.

Now, sitting on the balcony, feeling the soft breeze caress her skin, she thanked whatever god was looking out for her that she had.

"So, ready for some *colazione*?"

"Oooh – breakfast." Becky turned in her chair as the tall pilot pushed through the balcony doors bearing a small tray. She had changed from her uniform into a pair of jeans and a casual, short-sleeved white blouse.

"Well, its the best I could scrounge up from Signora Canova," she said, placing the tray down on the small all-weather table. "I don't think she likes me much. You should've seen the look she gave me."

"*I* would've liked to have seen the look *you* were giving *her,*" Becky said pointedly, softening her words with an arch smile.

"Hey," Kate protested, "I asked nicely. I'm sure I was smiling."

"Like you are now?"

"Well," a slightly furrowed brow, "yeah."

"Kate?" Becky gazed intently at the older woman.

"What?"

"You are *not* smiling."

"Well," Kate sniffed, easing herself down in the chair next to Becky. "What can I say? The *signora* brings out the best in me. We're lucky we got anything to eat at all," she said, waving her hand at the tray.

"Don't sell yourself short, Captain," Becky said, laughing. The tray was piled high with rolls, brioche, toast and jam, and two cappuccinos. "Some of your formidable charm must've gotten through. This is pretty good scrounging."

"Thanks," Kate said in a mollified tone. She reached out for a brioche. "Hey." She nibbled thoughtfully on the bun and pointed the remaining chunk of it towards Becky's feet, "Speaking of charm – nice shoes."

Becky followed Kate's gaze. On her left foot, she wore a dark brown slip-on, while the right foot featured an open-toed, putty colored skimmer. In the light of day, the difference between the two was obvious.

"Oh no," Becky groaned, immediately kicking off the offending footwear. "I was in a hurry... and I'd lost one of my shoes in the river... do you think anyone noticed?"

"Nah," Kate smirked, looking out over the *piazza* with sudden interest. "And anyway, if they did, they're halfway to New York by now. You'll never see 'em again."

"Riiiight." Becky shook her head and took a sip of her creamy cappuccino. "Until the next flight, that is." Becky deepened her voice, mimicking a passenger. "Oh, hello there, Miss. Glad to see you can dress yourself, now.'"

Both women laughed at that, with Catherine finally adding, "Don't you worry. They give you any trouble, you let me know."

The two new lovers proceeded to eat in silence for a time, simply enjoying the quiet company of one another and taking in the ever-changing sights and sounds of the square.

Coo – coo.

From the red-tiled roof above them a warbling pair of roosting pigeons suddenly took flight. The furious flapping of their wings as the hefty birds powered away reminded Kate of old newsreel footage she'd seen as a child; of the experimental aircraft that preceded the Wright Brothers' efforts. They were large and ungainly, with aerodynamics that seemed to defy all scientific laws of flight. And indeed, one after another, the planes had plummeted heavily to the earth, after a brief bittersweet taste of free flight. Or else they'd never gotten off the ground at all.

But not pigeons. Somehow, at the last moment, they were able to pull it all together and sustain their flight, hold their direction. No matter how out of control they first appeared.

Yes, Kate thought, those damn birds were survivors. And she was too, by God... a survivor. She deserved it: all of it. After all, hadn't Becky said so just a few short hours ago?

Catherine watched the young blonde happily munching on the last of a roll, slathering raspberry jam atop a slice of thick toast. How content the girl seemed now. If she hadn't come after her and stopped her from leaving... Kate's heart lurched at the thought. *And after how I treated her.*

A deep breath. "Rebecca—"

Green eyes lifted from the toast and studied the pilot.

"I – I'm sorry for the things I said." Kate released a sharp burst of air, and her shoulders sagged.

"I know."

God – was Hanson going to let her off that easy? The pilot pushed on. "It's just that... what I'm feeling," she turned away and squinted in the sunlight, not looking directly at Becky, "it overwhelms me. I'm not used to… that."

"Me too," Becky replied, reaching out her hand to cover Kate's own.

Catherine did not pull away from the touch. "But you're different, Rebecca. You're so… good. You deal with it. I'm not sure I know how. And yeah," she ran her free hand through her dark tresses, "it scares me."

Becky let her go on, sensing, knowing, that the troubled woman needed to explain somehow, as much for herself as for Becky. "When I feel that way – for any reason – even because of you – it triggers in me a part of myself I'm not very proud of. I – I don't want to hurt you again, Rebecca – I couldn't bear that." The pilot turned to the young flight attendant, her blue eyes misty in the ancient Roman sun.

"Lean on me, Kate," Becky said solemnly, giving the larger hand a squeeze. "I can take it."

The pilot looked at the flight attendant with a frank, appraising stare. "I do believe you can."

"That's right," Becky vowed with a wry grin, lightening the moment. "Just you try any more of that funny stuff." she menaced Kate with her right fist.

"Oh God, no." Kate shrank back in spite of herself, and began rubbing her jaw thoughtfully. "I think you loosened a tooth with that last one."

A sharp intake of air. "Did I?" Becky's voice was suddenly full of concern.

Kate continued to massage her jaw, moaning, before finally giving the young blonde a sidelong look and a wink. "Gotcha."

"Arrgh. You're worse than my nieces." Becky slammed her hand down on the armrest of her chair, sighing heavily. "Ah well, I guess I deserved that." She brushed a stray crumb off her lap and chuckled.

Kate's eyes suddenly turned into two flinty chips of blue diamonds. "You deserve the best, Rebecca. Of everything." The pilot paused awkwardly, as if realizing the profoundness of that statement. "Which reminds me," she continued, quickly hiding her discomfiture. "Get dressed."

"Wha—" Becky was startled at the pilot's sudden change in mood, watching her gather up the remains of their breakfast. She grabbed a last roll for the road. "What are we doing today?"

Kate lifted the tray and headed back through the balcony doors. "We're going on a picnic."

It was 30 minutes and two millennia from the Ausonia to Ostia Antica, the ancient seaport of Rome. The excavated town was now a government run archaeological site, lying in the grassy meadows between the Tiber River and the Tyrrhenian Sea.

Catherine made quick work of securing a basket and a blanket, provided by Signora Canova, to the back of the little Vespa.

"Wow," Becky observed, when she saw the picnic basket groaning with fruit, cheese, bread, cold veal patties, and wine. "I thought you said the *signora* didn't like you?"

"She doesn't," Kate replied while leaning over and strapping the blanket to the bike. "But I remembered that the other day she offered to put together a basket, so I held her to it. And once she knew you'd be coming along," a blue eye peered at Becky from between strands of loose, dark hair, "it was all over. She couldn't do enough... for you."

"You're welcome." Becky laughed, sliding on her helmet and climbing onto the rear of the scooter.

Soon the two women were whizzing along the Via del Mare towards Ostia, leaving the heavier, more congested traffic of Rome behind.

It was hard for the pilot to believe she was actually on her way to Ostia, for so many times she had literally flown past the ruined city on her way to Rome, and never taken the time to go there. She understood it to be one of the most remarkable and under-visited sites in all of southern Italy. Indeed, Signora Canova had told her that on this unusually warm weekday morning, so early in the tourist season, they were likely to have Ostia and the adjacent pine forest of Castelfusano all to themselves. And that was just fine with Kate. She didn't much feel like sharing Rebecca Hanson with anyone.

The nearness of the young woman sitting behind her, hanging on tightly, was exhilarating for the pilot. Becky hadn't said much since they hit the highway; the roaring breeze prevented that anyway, really. But Kate found herself highly attuned to Becky's slightest movements. She could feel her shift to take in a new sight, could tell when she saw something interesting by how she slightly tightened the grip she had on her waist; could sense her excitement and anticipation as Ostia Antica drew nearer and nearer.

It was as if Kate had known the little blonde for more than just a few days. Hell, Rebecca Hanson was doing such a job on the pilot's thawing heart that she felt as though she'd known the damn girl forever. And that was a good feeling, Kate decided, after a moment's consideration.

Still, thinking you know someone is one thing. The reality of it is another.

Kate had been wrong to leave Becky last night, and wildly presumptuous in her determination to make a decision for them both without consulting the young flight attendant. She knew that now. For Becky had set her straight, all right. In spades.

This 'relationship' thing is definitely new to me, Kate thought, as she tooled the Vespa up to a nearly empty parking area. She had much to learn. Not that she wasn't looking forward to some serious instruction in the matter from one Rebecca Hanson.

"Wow, check it out." Becky gasped, leaping off the back of the barely-stopped scooter, craning towards the entrance gate.

Kate grinned in spite of herself as she pulled off her helmet.

"It's like people still live here or something. Kate, you gotta see this – c'mon." the young blonde exhorted, before disappearing through the gate.

"Right behind ya, Champ." Kate shook her head, chuckling. "Right behind ya."

Signora Canova had been right. Ostia was nearly deserted. Unlike other tourist sites in Rome and its environs, there were no garishly colored tour buses, no clamoring crowds whose demanding shouts and cries sounded like a local meeting of the United Nations' Press Corps. The ancient buildings waited quietly, with a hint of a breeze blowing through their open roofs, windows, and foundations, greeting Kate and Becky with a low, welcoming 'hello'.

The two women opted to explore on their own, using only a map as their guide, preferring to take in the city on their own terms and timetable. And so Becky led the way, poring over the map and bobbing her head up periodically to ori-

ent herself. Kate trailed along next to her, backpack and blanket slung over one shoulder,
carrying the picnic basket.

Slowly, they walked through the deserted
streets of Ostia, marveling at buildings that
looked as though, with a few quick repairs, they
could be fully functional today. Thanks to the
protection of tidal silt and windblown sand, the
buried seaport had faded from memory and
remained hidden from the destructive hand of
progress until the beginning of the 20th century.
Now, under expert archaeological attention, supported by both local and international universi-
ties, Ostia came to life once again.

Kate and Becky strolled down the Decu-
manus Maximus, the main thoroughfare crossing
the city from end-to-end. Deep ruts still lined
the cobbled road, the only signs that remained of
the long-ago carts that had once clogged the *via.*

Structures that at one time housed temples,
taverns, and groceries, all built of stone and
brick, shared the roadside with columns of
spruce and pine trees. Lining the walkway like
silent sentries, the trees waved gently in the
breeze as the women passed by.

Arched entranceways and a fishnet pattern
to the brickwork were forms repeated in construction throughout the city, lending a distinct
sense of continuity and 'urban planning' to it all.
The early spring sun baked the quiet stones, and

the heated air slipped softly among the buildings and streets, raising a light, fine dust along its path.

Taking a turn off the main road, they proceeded past the Temple of Jupiter, through a rather smallish forum, and onto a road that housed what looked to be the ancient world's version of apartment buildings. Indeed, it was in these bricked, multi-story edifices where the common people – the merchants, sailors, and slaves of Ostia – lived and died.

"Wonder what the rent is on these things?" Becky's voice echoed oddly as they stopped in the cooler interior courtyard of a building.

"If you have to ask, you can't afford it." Kate grinned, admiring the long-ago ingenuity that conceived of the highly functional design of the residences. The particular inner courtyard where they stood had a number of second floor 'apartment' balconies that would've overlooked what once had been a communal cistern and swimming pool.

"Nice air conditioning, though."

The pilot smiled. "Must be that sea breeze."

Leaving the residential area behind, Becky and Kate walked to the thermal baths of Neptune. Here was Ostia's ancient gathering place for movers and shakers in the city. Deals were made, alliances forged, and fortunes won and lost – all under the guise of rest and relaxation in the healing, soothing waters of the baths. Inside the main bathing chamber, the young blonde gently traced her fingers over the edges of a huge, beautifully preserved mosaic of the sea god riding in his horse-drawn chariot.

"Some spa, huh?" Becky asked, looking over her shoulder at the tall pilot. "Can you imagine it?"

"Yeah," Kate replied matter-of-factly, lounging against the wall. "I can. And I think I would've passed on it."

"Figures." Becky pushed herself to her feet. "You need to learn how to relax, Kate."

"Oh, I know how to relax, all right," the older woman smirked at her young companion. "I just wouldn't have chosen to do it in here."

"Really?" Becky mused, leading the way back onto the street. "Too public?"

"Nope." Kate stuck her tongue in her cheek. "Too private." She held back a smile at the confusion that skipped across Becky's features.

"But these were public baths…"

"For men only."

"Wow." Becky animatedly paged through her guide, "Sex discrimination in the ancient world. Uh… how do you know that, Kate? It's not mentioned in here, not that I can see."

"I just know," Kate replied, gazing off into the distance. "Take my word for it. Although," she added, turning to grin at her friend, "if I really *had* wanted to get in here, 'men only' wouldn't have stopped me."

"I believe you," Becky laughed. "However..." she ran her eyes up and down the pilot's striking form, "I don't think a disguise would've done the trick."

"Nah," Kate chuckled, getting her drift. "I would've just barged in there and dared 'em to throw me out."

"Some dare," Becky said, for she knew all too well the formidable will of iron that was Catherine Phillips, when Kate was confronted with adversity.

Moving westward through the city, they stopped to peek inside the great amphitheater, looking for all the world as though it could host a production this very day on its small stage, with patrons filling the semi-circle of steep, stone bleachers rising up in front of it.

Finally, Kate and Becky stopped at the Marine Gate. One of three principal gates to the ancient town, this particular gate was once positioned next to the harbor and warehouses. Now, it stood more than a mile from a sea that eluded its grasp over a grassy, ancient tidal basin.

"What a difference a couple of millennia make, eh?" Kate casually reached out an arm, giving Becky's good shoulder a quick squeeze and release.

"Yeah," Becky softly agreed, lifting her head into the light, warm breeze that carried on it the salty tang of the ocean.

"Well," Kate said, rousing herself, "hungry?"

"What do *you* think?" Becky turned a twinkling green eye up to Kate, holding a hand against her stomach. "Can't you hear it?"

"I should have known," Kate grinned, motioning towards a grove of pines to the north. "Why don't we take a walk up there? Find a place to spread out?"

"Sounds like a plan." Becky swiped the blanket from Kate. "Let me carry this."

"No way," Kate insisted. "You're—"

"Kaaate…" Rebecca issued a stern warning with the tone of her voice. "Heel. I can carry this. I'm fine."

Kate fought down her better judgment and let the flight attendant have her way – that, and the fact that she had no desire to subject herself to another of Rebecca's right hooks. "Okay." She held her hand up in surrender. She dutifully followed the smaller woman across the meadow, and into the wooded groves of evergreens and sycamores that rose up out of the sloping, grass-covered ancient dunes.

Deeper and deeper Becky pressed into the forest, dissatisfied with every potential picnicking site that the pilot pointed out.

Finally, Kate had had enough. "Are we in Switzerland yet?"

"Hey – it was your idea to have a picnic," Becky retorted. "I just want to find a spot that – oh, wow," she gasped. At that moment, the forest fell away to reveal a grassy, open clearing, completely encircled by the woods as if to form nature's own *al fresco* dining room. Several large rocks dotted the ground, and a fair-sized stream meandered lazily along the edge of the glade, making its timeless, inexorable journey towards the sea.

Becky looked up at Kate and smiled. "We're here."

The women threw open the blanket next to a large rock under the speckled shade of an umbrella pine. Easing themselves down onto the ground, they quickly tucked into the *signora's* picnic basket.

"Now," Becky's stomach growled in delight, "let's see what Signora Canova packed for me."

"Tell me, were you *always* the teacher's pet?" Kate handed Becky a small glass and began to uncork a bottle of *Dolcetto,* a red wine from Piedmont, Italy's premier wine producing region.

"Yep." Becky smirked, watching the deep purple-colored liquid sparkle and shimmer as it filled her glass, absorbing the rays of sunlight like a prism.

"Well, here's to you, Champ," Kate laughed, clicking her glass against Becky's, "because it got us this nice spread. Cheers."

"Cheers." Becky took a sip of the wine, admiring its soft, fruity taste. "Mmmm. Nice. Now, what else ya got in there?" She reached an arm across the pilot's midriff, and grabbed for a loaf of thick-crusted Italian bread.

"Hey, leave some for me." Kate playfully slapped at Becky's hand, and proceeded to liberate the contents of the basket. Melon, grapes, strawberries, two kinds of cheeses, cold breaded veal patties wrapped in wax paper, a bottle of Pelligrino water, and a slab of iced orange sponge cake.

Becky was stunned. "Wait until I see the *signora,*" she proclaimed, holding up a little silver fork and linen napkin. "This is amazing."

"No wonder the basket was so heavy." Kate leaned back against the rock and kicked her long legs out in front of her. "But I'm sure," she eyed Becky digging into the cheese and bread, "we won't have that problem on the way back."

The women ate their fill and then some. They talked little, enjoying instead the serenade of the woodland: the breathing whisper of the wind through the trees, the chattering of the crickets, the calling of the songbirds, the soft, throbbing hum of the forest. It was all around them, its life force seeping unbidden into their bodies.

"I'm stuffed," Becky sighed at last, placing a vine, plucked clean of grapes, onto her plate. "How about a break before dessert?" she suggested, squirming her way next to the pilot.

Kate did not protest. "Sure." She put down her wine glass and dropped her arm around Becky's shoulders, as though it were the most natural thing in the world to do. "We have time."

The dark-haired woman breathed in deeply. She let her eyes lazily wander past the pair of shapely legs revealed by Becky's khaki shorts, down towards a pair of yellow and white butterflies, playing and fluttering against one another just past her companion's naked feet.

"This is nice," Becky said softly, her senses pinging at the nearness of the pilot.

"Mm-hmm," Kate agreed, wondering how it could be that the blonde mop of hair nestled in the crook of her shoulder carried on it the scent of pine needles and honeysuckle.

"Hey, look." Becky's voice was a hoarse whisper, as she pointed towards an aged sycamore standing about 20 yards away. A small, robin-sized bird, painted with the colors of the rainbow, was busily pecking away at a hollow in the trunk of the tree. "I wonder if she's making a nest?"

"*He* is probably looking for something good to eat," Kate said archly.

"Oh, where's your sense of romance," Becky grumbled, giving her companion a gentle poke in the ribs.

Two could play at this game, the pilot resolved. "I got you on this picnic, didn't I?" And she gave the top of the golden head a quick kiss.

Becky pushed herself up with her hands, and swiveled so she could look the pilot in the eye. "Yeah, you did." She smiled a little, and turned slightly as the rainbow bird took off. "Look, there she goes."

"He," Kate corrected, teasing the young blonde.

"I wonder where *it's* going," Becky countered, watching the flash of color as the bird disappeared into the wood. "Where it's been… if it's looking for a mate—"

"Or found one." Kate's blue eyes twinkled.

"If it is new to this…" Becky waved a hand around the clearing, "place, or has been nesting here for years? Does it have any family? What will the future hold for it?"

"Geez, Hanson." Kate levered herself higher against the rock, struggling to keep her voice light. She was afraid she knew where this conversation was going. "Firing off all those brain cells over some bird?"

"Kate," green eyes locked onto blue in a level, unflinching gaze, "I want to know all there is to know about you. Everything. I don't want you to hold anything back. What is a part of you is a part of me."

"Okaaay." Kate ran a hand uncomfortably through her hair. "I had a feeling we weren't just bird-watching."

"Catherine Phillips," Becky's eyes grew dark and stormy, "you know damn well what I'm talking about."

"I do... I do," Kate soothed, pulling Becky back in close to her, stroking her hair. "It's just... you know it won't come pouring out at once, Rebecca. And I feel the same way about you, too – believe me. I want to know it all. Good, bad, and indifferent."

"Yeah," Becky said. "But one of us is more quiet than Mount Rushmore, and one of us, well, there are times I feel as though I'm prattling my head off about stuff that nobody cares about, and I wish I could stop myself but I can't... because when it's too quiet I get real nervous and that only makes me want to talk more, just to fill the silence—" She paused to take in a heaving breath. "Like now, for instance." Becky released a frustrated, choking laugh.

"I don't mind that," Kate said softly, giving the smaller woman a squeeze. "Your voice is like... music to my soul."

Becky twisted again to look up at Kate, blinking. "Really?"

"Really," Kate assured her. And then, to prove she meant it, added, "Go on."

"Okay." Becky bit her lower lip, hesitant. "Kate," she gently inquired, "tell me about your brother. The one who died."

Shit! An icy thunderbolt shot through Catherine, and she felt her stomach suddenly twist into a hot poker of a knot. It was a sensation she knew well. She felt it every time she allowed herself to think back about her fair-haired little brother. About what had happened to him… how he died. More and more it was his tragic end that dominated her thoughts, thoroughly overshadowing the good times they'd shared, and Kate was powerless to stop it, allowing herself to be carried along on that shield of suffering.

Perhaps it was because when he was killed, she'd lost that final thread of a link to what anyone might consider a home or family... with no one but herself to blame.

Funny thing, though – as Rebecca continued to study her, reaching out a hand and placing it on Kate's own, she felt that… pain, that hurt, start to recede a bit. Strange. Very strange.

"You mean Brendan."

"Was that his name?"

"Yeah," Kate sighed, pushing tired, tense air out of her lungs. She was not unhappy to let it go. Perhaps it had overstayed its welcome. "Brendan Thomas Phillips," she said, in a voice struggling to maintain its composure. "He was my little brother. And I loved him."

It poured out of Catherine, all of it, in a raging torrent, unleashed. How they'd been best friends as children, competitive siblings during adolescence, and the pride she'd felt when he'd decided as a young man to follow her into the Air Force. How even though he didn't make it into the Academy as she had, he still kept at it; enrolling in Air Force ROTC while attending college, getting his commision upon graduation, then moving through the ranks on his own.

All her life, it had been Brendan and her against the world, against the hurt of their father's passing and their mother's indifference, against the stoic coldness of their older brother, Peter. So much like their mother. And how they loved to poke fun at the stuffy Air Force hierarchy. They themselves would never be that way, of course, once they received their stars.

And then – just like that – he was gone. Killed, in the crash of an experimental version of the F-16. Pilot error, the Air Force had called it.

In a freaking experimental craft? No. No way. Brendan was too good for that. He hadn't gotten disoriented and dizzy, the result of jamming the throttle forward into full afterburner one time too many. Confused, he hadn't accidentally rolled his plane into an inverted spin, drilling into the ground outside Edwards like a 12-ton pile driver. If only that joke of a hearing panel had let her see all the paperwork... she knew there was more to the story. There had to be.

But all her protests, her efforts to get to the bottom of it, had met with a stony wall of silence. She'd owed it to Brendan to uncover the truth… owed it to herself, as if that would have alleviated even a single ounce of the guilt she felt for ever having urged him to pursue his dream in the first place.

A dream that got him killed.

"It's not your fault, you know," Becky said fiercely, pushing the dark hair from the pilot's slightly lowered face.

Kate raised watery, reddened eyes to her young friend. "I *know* it, but I don't *feel* it," she cried, striking a fist onto her chest. "Not in here."

"He made his choices, Kate, just as you did. What if it had been the other way around? What if you'd gotten the test pilot's assignment? What then?"

"That's different—"

"Not really." Becky's voice was stern. "What if it had been you? If you'd been the one who had died?" A shiver of fear snaked through the flight attendant at that dark thought. "Would you want Brendan to go sleepwalking though life, choking on the responsibility… on the guilt… that he'd gotten you killed?"

"No." Kate nearly shouted. "That would be ridiculous."

"Why?" Becky demanded. "Why would it?"

"Because." The pilot felt her body stiffening under Rebecca's cross-examination. Damn it, why didn't the girl back off?

"Tell me, Kate." Becky lifted her hand to turn the older woman's face towards her. "Why?"

"Because." And then the tears began to flow. "Because… it would've been my choice. Mine. Not his."

"That's right… that's right." Becky leaned into the pilot now, pulling her trembling body close. "He made his choice, Kate. And you did too. We all do. How about giving him a little credit for that, huh?"

If there was one thing Catherine Phillips had learned over the past few days, it was to listen when Rebecca Hanson was talking. Because she'd found out more often than not, that the determined young woman usually made sense. Most of the time, anyway.

And now, after having talked about events… feelings, that were still so raw within her, the pilot discovered that there might be a chance, however slim, that the wound might begin heal. She would always bear the scar, she owed that to Brendan's memory, but life, for her, could go on. In Rebecca Hanson, she'd found the reason. Even now, the woman's soothing voice calmed her… offered a gentle touch, held her demons at bay.

"You know," Kate said, her voice a near whisper, "when I got on that plane in New York, I was quitting. I'd sent a resignation letter off to Cyrus and everything."

Kate felt the younger woman tense in her arms, and then pull away. "What?" Green eyes flew open in wonder, gazing up at the pilot. "Everything you did on that plane... how you risked your life... and you were *quitting?*"

"Yeah. It just didn't seem to matter any more. None of it."

"You... you..." Becky groped for the right words, fearing what she might hear.

A hint of a smile played at Catherine's lips. "I told Cyrus I'd made a mistake," she explained, "back when you were still in the hospital."

"Wow." Becky shook her head, trying to process it all. "What changed your mind?"

The pilot answered without hesitation. "You." *What the hell.* After all, it was true wasn't it?

Becky remained silent for a moment, absorbing the gravity of what she'd just heard. And then, without a word, she leaned in and brushed her lips delicately against the pilot's own, pleased at the slight tremor she felt run through them at the contact.

She kissed Kate again, lingering this time, daring her to stop the palm she slipped inside her white button-down blouse. She was not barred, and Becky was astonished at the heat she felt as she gently touched the smooth skin there.

"No... not here," Kate weakly groaned, but Rebecca already knew from the way the taller woman was responding to her caresses that she held the upper hand.

"We haven't seen another soul for hours, and you know it." She peppered kisses down Kate's neck, delighting at how the pilot arched her chin upwards, tacitly granting unobstructed access to the soft, tanned flesh of her throat.

"You sure?" Kate's voice was hoarse as she silently answered her own question, shifting away from the rock and lying back on the blanket, taking Becky with her.

The blonde flight attendant levered herself up on one arm, temporarily blocking the sun from the pilot's view. "Captain," she intoned in a low, sultry voice, "I'm going to show you just what you decided to stay for."

And with that, she began a merciless assault on Catherine Phillips, using skills that were untested and new, but expertly guided by the want, the desire, the love that burned within her. She could sense Kate holding back at first, hesitant, fussing when she reached for the buttons of her blouse... the snap of her jeans.

But Becky was relentless in her mission, driving her body against Kate's, her breathing intimately in sync with the taller woman's beneath her. Blissfully, she took in the intoxicating scent of her, insistent that her hands, her lips, her tongue, be given the freedom to roam as she saw fit upon Kate's body.

To feel. To taste. To touch.

With each new kiss, with each newly dis-covered territory, Becky's passion burned brighter and brighter, until finally she could see nothing but the sun, and she and Kate were in it, glowing in the heat, in the fire, burning hot. And when she heard a strangled cry, felt large fingers tightly entwine with her own, she knew that Kate had surrendered at last.

Success. Becky thought, as joy flooded through her. Tears dampened her face as she eased herself down into Kate's welcoming arms. This first battle, she had won. Little did she realize as a blue eye winked open at her, that the battle had barely begun.

Shadows began to deepen in the glade as the sun continued its march across the sky. There were several hours of daylight remaining, but the golden orb had passed its apex and now reached its slanted fingers down through the trees and onto the blanket where Kate and Becky lay.

"Phew," Kate gasped, falling back onto the blanket, perspiring heavily. Still, she kept one heated hand on Becky's firm stomach. "Did we make up yet?"

"I don't know." Becky struggled for air herself, as rivulets of sweat coursed down her body. "I think I'm still a little mad—"

"Youuuu." With a deep-throated growl, Kate rolled over and pinned Becky to the blanket, silencing her with a searing kiss.

"Okay... okay..." Becky shrieked when at last the pilot released her. "We've made up. Any more of this staying mad is gonna kill me."

"Yeah." Smoky blue eyes bored into green. "But what a way to go." With a devilish grin, Kate slapped Becky lightly on the hip. "C'mon. Let's go." And she was off.

"Kate, wha—" Words suddenly failed the flight attendant at the stunning sight of Kate's lithe, naked form moving confidently across the clearing. Suddenly, she disappeared from view, followed by a great *splash.*

She didn't, Becky thought to herself. *She wouldn't.*

And then, a dark, water-slicked head and shoulders rose up from the bank of the stream. "C'mon in." Gleaming white teeth flashed in a smile. "Water's fine."

"No. No way." Becky retorted, even as she felt herself rising and moving towards Kate, returning her smile with a broad, silly one of her own. The pilot was crazy. Okay, so she felt hot and sweaty, but she would have none of this cavorting naked in a strange stream with this wild woman. Not her. No sir.

Splash!

Later, they'd dried off nibbling on the orange sponge cake and on each other, taking sips of the Pelligrino water in between. Kate had pulled the blanket back out of the afternoon sun that had invaded their shade and, after they'd slipped back into their clothes, the pilot did not protest when the smaller woman slid up against her and her eyes fluttered shut.

"Just... a few minutes..." Becky had mumbled, and Kate was more than content to let her sleep. To dream.

Now, she contentedly watched the sun dip lower towards the tips of the trees lining the western side of the glade. She would let Becky rest for a few moments, but then, she thought reluctantly, they would have to leave this place.

In the peaceful hum of the forest, with the stream softly gurgling in the distance and Rebecca by her side, Catherine found herself marveling once again at how comfortable, how familiar the young woman seemed to her. There was such an element of certainty... of destiny about it all, standing in such stark contrast to the pure, rotten luck that had thrown them together in the first place.

Maybe it was because they lay under a sky that had watched the ancients come and go, and upon ground that still echoed with the footsteps of those who had gone before – people who had lived, loved, and died here. In the stillness, in the in-between breaths, Kate swore she could feel those spirits around her now. If she closed her eyes, she was certain she could even hear them... see them, rising up from the darkened shadows of the forest...

"Grrrrrzzzzz-pffft-zzsssh!"

Kate's eyes ripped open, and she jolted to a sitting position. How long had she been asleep? Not long, she judged, checking out the sun's position in the sky. Breathing hard, she swung her eyes down to Becky. In spite of the sudden movement, the girl continued to snooze happily away.

"Grrrrrzzzzz-pffft!"

That Hanson, Kate smiled, *she's better than an alarm clock.*

"Hey." The pilot carefully shook Becky's shoulder, just as another ungodly snore caused a flock of sparrows to take off from the trees to their left.

"Hrrmpf..."

"Let's go, Champ," Kate chuckled, "before we get stuck here."

"And that would be bad because... why?" Becky gazed fuzzily at the pilot from beneath the crook of an arm she'd flung across her forehead.

"I can see I'll have to persuade you," Kate replied, eyes flashing. She dropped her lips to

Rebecca's own, pressing her case. She intended
to take as long as necessary to make the young
flight attendant understand. For here, in this forgotten glade within an ancient Roman forest,
time had no meaning.

It was a race between the Vespa and the setting sun during the entire return trip along the
Via del Mare to Rome. Catherine was determined to get herself and Rebecca back to the
Ausonia while there was still daylight left, not
having any great desire to test the little scooter
against local drivers on a high-speed *autostrada*
after dark. Fortunately, more of the traffic at this
hour seemed to be heading the opposite direction, leaving Rome.

They would make it just in time, Kate
thought, as the Eternal City loomed in front of
her, its sun-bleached buildings bathed in the rust
and copper tones of the dying sun. She hadn't
intended to stay out this late, had never planned
to allow herself to get so… distracted. But now,
feeling Rebecca's arms cinched around her
waist, the slight pressure against her back as the
tired girl leaned into her, the pilot did not regret
a bit of it.

In fact, it was quite the contrary. Catherine
Phillips had never had so idyllic a day as this.
Spending time with someone, a lover, who she
cared about so desperately, so passionately, so

completely. Someone, who, Kate dared to hope, felt the same way about her.

Rebecca Hanson.

Catherine sang the name in her heart. This extraordinarily giving woman who wanted nothing in return. With Rebecca, there was no hidden agenda, no ulterior motive, no coldly animalistic, disassociated lust. The young blonde cared for her, gave herself to her, simply because she *wanted* to. No one, but no one, had ever done that for her before. Maybe, if she was honest with herself, Kate considered, it was because she'd never let anyone get close enough to try.

But Rebecca Hanson was not just anyone. She was a someone. *Her* someone. And something about that felt very, very right.

In no time at all, Kate had maneuvered the Vespa through the city, back up the Via del Corso, finally taking a last sweeping turn onto the Via du Macelli. Arriving at the Ausonia, the pilot steered the bike into a small scooter space just to the right of the *pensione's* front door.

"Boy am I beat." Becky yawned, stepping slowly, unsteadily to her feet from the back of the scooter. "All that fresh air, sunshine—"

"And exercise," Kate winked, doffing her helmet.

"Sure beats the inside of a plane," the flight attendant finished, unperturbed. "But I can barely keep my eyes open."

"No problem." Kate eyed her companion carefully. The girl did look a bit flushed. Perhaps they *had* overdone it today. "We can just sack out early—"

"But we're still gonna have dinner, aren't we?" Becky rubbed her eyes sleepily.

"Yeah," Kate laughed, shaking her head. "I wouldn't think of having you miss a meal. I'd never hear the end of it. Literally." She poked the smaller woman gently in the stomach.

"Now you're talking," Becky said, brightening at the prospect of another dining experience. "I could go for pasta tonight... or maybe some seafood..."

Becky proceeded to rattle off a litany of potential food selections, growing more awake and alert by the moment. Kate released a soft, amazed chuckle, and moved to the rear of the scooter to unstrap the basket and backpack. The girl's appetite was ferocious. Kate shuddered at the thought of what might happen if she ever got between Rebecca Hanson and a good meal.

The dark pilot listened to Becky chatter on while she tugged at a balky strap on the bike. Out of the corner of her eye, she noticed a couple, casually dressed in jeans and t-shirts, exit the front doors of the Ausonia. A small, white terrier skittered out behind them before the doors swung closed. The couple was clearly caught by surprise as the excited pup darted between their feet, causing them to stumble and nearly fall.

But the little dog paid them no heed, joyfully reveling in his newfound freedom.

Without a sideways glance, the terrier promptly darted straight out into the middle of the still busy Via du Macelli.

"Oh…" Becky strangled her dining commentary to a stop. She had seen it too.

"Hey! Doggie! What are you doing?" The man stepped in front of his female companion and called after the dog.

But the terrier was caught between opposing lanes of traffic now, and seemed unsure of what to do. Hesitantly, it looked back over its shoulder towards the doors of the Ausonia, and waggled its head.

"He's gonna get hit…" Becky shrieked in a high-pitched, worried voice.

Kate started moving towards the street.

The wild screeching of brakes and angry bleating of horns only served to confuse the dog further, and he began to pitifully whine and shake.

Just then, a flash of color flew out the doors of the *pensione.*

"Pepitto!"

That did it. The little pup started to trot back across the street, moving like a fish on a line towards the voice that had called him. Unfortunately, that course took him directly into the path of a speeding, swerving Alfa Romeo.

"Pepitto – NO!"

The sports coupe hurtling towards the dog was fast, but Catherine Phillips was faster. In a blur of arms, legs, and fur, Kate lunged out into the roadway, scooping the dog up one-handed.

The Alfa was nearly on top of them now, barreling out of control. It was impossible to get out of the way in time, that much was apparent. Becky's mouth fell open in a silent scream.

Off balance as she was, Kate somehow found the leverage to plant her left foot solidly and push herself off in a violent roll towards the sidewalk. The terrified dog pawed furiously at her chest as she pulled him in, cradling him.

Kate tumbled away from the swerving car, feeling the heat of its engine in her face and tasting the burned rubber of its tires as it passed within millimeters of her.

"Kaaaate!"

The pilot rolled to a stop next to the curb and looked up to see a stricken Rebecca running towards her. Also nearly upon her was the flash of color from the Ausonia.

Signora Canova.

The proprietress was wearing yet another wildly designed smock-dress that looked like a Picasso canvas gone bad.

"Pepitto! Pepitto!" she cried out, reaching for the trembling dog.

With a groan, Kate pushed herself to her feet. "This little runaway belong to you?"

"Oh... Miss Phillips... *grazie! Grazie!* How can I ever thank you?" She took Pepitto in her arms, letting loose a stream of Italian endearments and loving rebukes that even Kate was hard-pressed to follow.

"Don't mention it," Kate said, brushing herself off.

"Good God, Kate, are you okay?" Becky gave the taller woman a hug and then pulled back. "You scared the heck out of me. And look at your arm."

Kate followed Becky's gaze to her right elbow. It was badly skinned and bleeding.

"I'm fine," Kate assured her. "Just have to clean it up a bit."

"You come inside right now, Miss Phillips, I take care of you after I put Pepitto back." She returned her attention to her dog. "You never, never to go out alone, eh?" She wagged her finger at him. "But those bad people, they open the doors in front of you and off you go like a rocket."

"You're okay now, Pepitto," Becky said, reaching out and ruffling the dog's head. The pup gave her hand a quick lick with its pink tongue.

"Bad people," the *signora* repeated, nodding towards where a small crowd of onlookers had gathered. "They say they are friends of yours, Miss Hanson, but I no believe it." And at that, the proprietress flounced back indoors.

"Uhhhh…" followed by a nervous cough. "Surprise, you guys."

The couple who had freed Pepitto was Nathan Berbick and Cindy Walters, Orbis flight attendants whose most recent journey with Kate and Rebecca had been on the ill-fated flight 2240. Afterwards, they'd decided to spend a few days layover in Rome, rekindling their on again, off again relationship.

"Well," Nathan shifted from his right foot to his left, and thrust his hands into his jeans pockets, "who wants some dinner?"

"Are you sure that shoulder's feeling okay, hon?" Cindy Walters searched the green eyes of her friend as the rickety lift climbed to the Ausonia's fifth floor. "You had us so worried."

"I'm fine Cin," Becky said, stealing a quick sidelong look at her suddenly silent pilot. "Really." Once they'd entered Ausonia, Becky had been amazed at how the *signora* couldn't seem to do enough for Kate, clucking over her skinned elbow with antiseptic and bandages, profusely swearing her thanks all the while. It had taken some doing for the pilot to finally extricate herself from the *signora's* grateful, effusive clutches.

"Yeah, you gave us quite a scare," Nathan said, running a hand through his closely cropped hair. "Glad to see you're doing so good."

"And how do you feel – ah – Captain?" Cindy asked, fumbling over how to address Becky's tall, imposing traveling companion.

"Never better." Kate gazed at the dimly lit floor indicator of the elevator, willing it towards its destination, hastening its journey. This unexpected company had thrown her off balance, and she didn't like it one bit.

Suddenly, she felt a sharp pressure on her foot.

Looking down to determine its source, she was surprised to see green orbs glaring up at her. *"Captain?"*

"Oh," she smiled faintly. "Call me… Catherine. Please."

Becky arched an eyebrow at Kate, but let it pass. The lift jolted to a stop. "Wait until you see the room," she enthused as the taller woman slid the gate open.

A quick walk down the plush, carpeted hall, and then the young blonde proudly flung open the door. "Check this out."

"Oh wow." Cindy's voice was breathless as she swooped into the room, running her hands over the furniture and fabrics, tracing the lines of the mouldings. "Incredible."

"Not too bad," Nathan added, clearly impressed by the sumptuous décor, the spectacular view, and the cloud-like canopy bed. "How much you paying for this?" He grabbed an apple from the fresh fruit basket and crashed down backwards across the billowing white comforter.

"100,000 lire." Becky sat down into a chair near the window, crossing a leg under herself.

"Whaaat?" Cindy's shriek might have been heard across the Tiber. "Nathan, aren't we paying five times that at the Hilton?"

"Yeah," Nathan took a crunching bite of apple, "but at least we don't have to deal with a dragon lady of a hotel clerk." He pushed himself up onto his elbows. "What's up with her?"

"Now darlin', she wasn't that bad." Cindy playfully slapped him on the top of his head. "Just a bit... eccentric. And you *did* let her doggie out."

"I did not," Nathan protested. "You did. You saw the Captain... er... Catherine and Becky pulling in, and made a beeline for the doors."

"Well, you followed me quickly enough," the petite brunette reasoned.

Nathan sat up and tossed his apple core into the wastebasket near the desk. It thunked loudly as it hit bottom. "No kidding. I couldn't wait to get out of there. The way she kept staring... nasty."

"I think she's sweet," Becky said, shrugging her shoulders. "She's been wonderful to us."

"To *you*," came a muffled voice from the closet where Kate was stowing their backpack.

"I don't know about that," Becky chuckled and shoved herself to her feet. "After you rescued Pepitto—"

"That mutt…" Nathan mumbled.

"Terrier –" Becky corrected, "– you certainly were the apple of her eye."

"Speaking of apples… any more?" The lean, dark-eyed man glanced hopefully at the basket.

"Naaathan," Cindy warned in her soft, Southern drawl, "you'll spoil your appetite."

"Yeah, anyway," the young flight attendant reluctantly got up from the bed, "we thought we'd drop by and surprise you… you know, take you to dinner. First and last chance, since we're going home on the early flight tomorrow."

"Is this a bad time?" Cindy linked her arm in Nathan's.

Kate was just closing the closet door and turned around at that remark.

"Well…"

"No, of course not," Becky jumped in, shooting the pilot a dark, warning look. "We were just about to go get something to eat. Right, Kate?"

The pilot smiled tightly, desperately thinking good thoughts. "Riiiight."

Passetto was a fairly good-sized restaurant situated on the Via Boncompagni, within easy

walking distance of the Pensione Ausonia.
Reluctantly, Signora Canova had given Nathan
the recommendation after finally recognizing
that the evil people who'd nearly gotten her Pepitto killed *had* to have something to eat. That,
and the fact that it appeared they were friends of
the delightful Rebecca Hanson and the brave,
wonderful Catherine Phillips after all.

The restaurant was in an older building, and
featured battered tables and a faded maroon car-
pet, spattered with stains. But what the estab-
lishment lacked in décor and ambiance, it made
up for in the quality of its cuisine: an intriguing
menu, ample portions, and the best-tasting food
the pilot had ever eaten in Rome.

Kate noticed that the patrons seemed to be a
blend of locals and tourists alike, with the wait-
staff operating more quickly than the norm in
other Italian eateries. Good. The sooner they
were out of here and ditched Berbick and
Walters, the better. Who had invited them to
intrude, anyway? But they were Rebecca's
friends so… she'd try to make the best of it, she
decided.

After all, without Nathan's help, and Alan
Ross's too, for that matter, that bastard of a
hijacker might've gotten away with it, and killed
them all. But that didn't mean now that the traumatic event was over with, Catherine had to
spend time with them. Her time was limited, she

had a choice, and dammit – she wanted Rebecca all to herself.

So maybe she was being a bit childish, she thought, as the dishes came and went and the wine flowed. But better to say nothing than to say something that... well, that 'Captain Frosty' might say, and so she mostly kept her mouth shut and concentrated on her pork scaloppini, lavished with capers, white wine, sage and prosciutto.

Becky was having a good time, that was all that mattered, she told herself. The young blonde's face was flushed, probably from both the excitement and the wine. Kate had spoken up only once – overriding Nathan's wine selection and demanding that they opt for a Trentino Valpolicella, instead. *It was the better wine, after all,* Kate rationalized, reaching for another sip and relishing the smooth heat of it sliding down her throat. *Yep. Good stuff.* She poured herself another glass.

"Oh, me too." Becky pushed her empty glass towards Kate. "Please?" she smiled, hiccuping.

"Good thing you're not driving, Champ." Nathan covered his glass with his hand when Kate mutely offered him more. He hadn't liked the pilot's choice in wine, and by God, the way 'Frosty' was acting tonight, he wasn't much sure he liked *her* either. Not that Becky appeared to notice. What had come over her? It was as if, in her eyes, Phillips could do no wrong.

"You sure you've been okay?" Cindy pushed away her plate of antipasto, reached across the table, and gave Becky's arm a squeeze. "I just can't believe it. After everything that happened…"

"I feel… fantastic, if you must know," Becky said, twirling a forkful of spaghetti in lobster sauce. "These last few days have been wonderful."

"Nobody's bothered you… you know, the press or anything?"

"Yeah," Nathan said. "They were camped out in the lobby of the Hilton for a couple of days, before they lost interest in us, I think."

"We haven't been hassled by anybody, have we Kate?"

"Nope."

"Well, all hell is breaking loose stateside." Nathan put his arm around Cindy's shoulders. "People want to know how this happened."

"A goddamned loser with a gun and a bomb, who tricked a few poor saps into following him, that's how it happened."

A shocked silence fell over the table at the sudden outburst from the pilot.

"Well, it's the truth, isn't it?" Kate took another sip from her glass, and narrowed her eyes at her companions.

"Anyway," Nathan cleared his throat, "Orbis is in really hot water now, with the security breach and all."

"So, where have y'all been sightseeing?" Cindy's voice was high and shrill, as she desperately sought to change the subject. The last thing she wanted to see was an ugly argument break out between the captain and her Nathan. For Becky's sake, more than anything else. The young Californian was acting as though she'd known Catherine Phillips forever, instead a little under a week.

"Oh gosh." Becky pulled a small plate filled with artichokes simmered in olive oil closer to her. "Rome has been wonderful. We've been everywhere... done everything."

"Like what?" Cindy pressed. She leaned into the table and plaited her fingers in front of her.

"Yeah, tell us," Nathan said, grinning at Cindy. "We didn't get out much."

"Nathan." Cindy gave her boyfriend a sharp poke in the ribs. "Really."

"Well..." Becky began, "we went shopping, went on a walking tour... the Forum and the Colosseum were awesome."

"Except for the mugging," Kate muttered.

"And then Kate rented a scooter—"

"What?" Cindy's eyes flew open wide. "Those things are dangerous."

"Not with Kate. She has a Harley, you know." Becky happily reached for her wineglass.

"Oh. How... nice," Cindy said, gulping. Proper young women in Charleston wouldn't be caught dead on the back of a motorcycle. It figured that this Catherine Phillips would be a bit rough around the edges.

Shit, Kate inwardly groaned, and began admiring the dead moths in a ceiling light fixture. *Hanson, I need to have a conversation with you later about too much personal disclosure.*

"And then we went to see the Appian Way... the Trevi Fountain... the Vatican... gosh, I'm forgetting – what else, Kate?"

"Nearly drowning in the Tiber?" Kate helpfully suggested.

"Yeah – there was this fantastic club on a river barge with music and stuff, and then... oh, I wish I could remember it all now, but – oh yes – today we went on a picnic."

"Well, you look like you got some sun, Champ," Nathan said, playfully plucking at her nose.

"Did I ever," Becky snorted. She opened her mouth to add to the story, but Kate cut her off before she incriminated herself further.

"Tomorrow we're going to the Pantheon." The pilot forced a benign smile.

"Are we?" Becky squealed, "That'll be great. And some more shopping? Can we? I still need to get something for my parents, and Eileen and her husband, and Johnny, and of course maybe some more stuff for my nieces..."

Kate swung her eyes to Nathan. "Did you get the check?"

"Not yet," he said, poking with his fork at the remnants of grilled baby lamb chops.

"Oh, don't let's go yet," Becky cried. "Did you see those fried, cheese-filled ravioli, drizzled with honey? I want to try some."

"Waiter." Nathan flagged down a passing *cameriere* and placed the order. Anything for Becky Hanson. She was a good girl, one of the nicest he'd ever flown with. Her new buddy was another matter.

"I still can't get over your room," Cindy said, shaking her brunette head. "And the price."

"How about that bed, huh?" Becky winked. "It's like out of a dream."

"And huge," Nathan added, "so at least you're not on top of each other."

"Oh, you'd be surprised," Becky giggled. "It's not as big as you'd think."

Kate closed her eyes and swore she could see bright, pulsing laser bursts shooting across her lids. *For the love of God*, she wondered, *will dessert ever get here?*

Finally, Rebecca Hanson had gotten enough to eat. Or perhaps the restaurant had simply run out of food... Kate couldn't be sure. After they paid the check, Nathan and Cindy ordered up a taxi to take them back to the Hilton.

"We can drop you off," Cindy offered. "You're along the way."

"No," the dark-haired woman quickly declined for the both of them, "We're just around the corner," her voice was firm, "and the fresh air will do us good, right?" She shifted to take in Rebecca's flushed, upturned features.

"Um... right." Becky chirruped, happy to agree with anything her pilot suggested. "Wanna walk with us?"

Kate held her breath.

"Nah," Nathan eyed Catherine warily, "the cab's already on its way."

"Taxi... taxi." The maitre'd scurried over to their table and motioned towards the front door.

Kate led the way outside, only too glad to leave the stifling environment of Passetto behind.

A squat Fiat cab sat idling on the Via Bon-compagni, its middle-aged, smoking driver peering at them through the window.

"Well, see you back home." Cindy gave Becky a hug. "Take care of yourself, okay?" She searched the blonde flight attendant's eyes. "Be careful."

"I will, Cin." A broad grin flashed across Becky's face. "Don't worry."

"See you soon, Champ." Nathan stepped up, circled his arm around Becky's shoulders, and gave her a quick peck on the cheek.

"Bye, Nathan." Becky's eyes were moist. "And thanks... for everything."

The dark, handsome young man swallowed hard. "You're welcome, kiddo."

"Okay..." Nathan and Cindy turned towards Kate. The pilot stood stock-still with her hands firmly clasped behind her back.

"So long," Kate offered, unmoving.

"Good-bye, Cap... er... Catherine." Cindy blushed at the awkwardness of the moment.

"Yeah, see ya," Nathan said without emotion, turning away from Kate to open the door of the taxi.

A flurry of final good-byes and waves, and the tail lights of the cab disappeared into the Roman night.

Kate gently propelled Becky back in the direction of the Ausonia, falling into step beside her.

The younger woman sighed happily. "It was great to see them, wasn't it?"

"Mm-hmm," Kate rumbled.

Becky studied her new lover carefully. It had not escaped her notice that the pilot had clammed up for most of the meal, save for a few stark blasts of commentary. Well, she really

hadn't known Nathan and Cindy too well...
maybe that was it. Still, the two flight attendants
were her friends, and she wanted them to like
Catherine as much as she did. And vice versa.

Somehow, she thought, as she walked in
silence next to the older woman, the evening had
fallen somewhat short of that goal. Kate wasn't
angry... not exactly, she could tell that much.
But as she stole a glance at the pilot's tight, chis-
eled features, she knew that her demeanor had
definitely changed from the open, accessible
state she'd been in earlier.

Before Nathan and Cindy had arrived,
Becky glumly realized.

It was late when they re-entered the Ausonia, and Becky felt the weight of her active day,
the rich meal, and the wine creeping into her
bones, tugging down at her eyelids.

Of course, Signora Canova was at her station behind the front desk. A *sigaretta* dangled
from her thin lips, and she peered over the top of
her pince-nez to take in the new arrivals.

"Miss Hanson! Miss Phillips!" She grabbed
at the cigarette and quickly extinguished it.
"How you like Passetto*?* Is good, eh?" A wide,
welcoming smile displayed two rows of tiny,
narrow teeth.

"Dinner was great, thanks," Becky said,
grinning through a yawn.

"Miss Phillips, how you feel? Your arm?" The *signora* scurried out from behind the desk, reaching for Kate.

"Fine… just fine, thanks." Kate shied away. "Really."

"Okaaay," the *signora* said doubtfully, planting her hands on her hips and staring up at the taller woman. "You want *colazione* in your room again tomorrow? I bring."

"No… no…" Kate held up her hand. "We'll come down to eat. Thank you anyway." The last thing she wanted now was the newly friendly *signora* in their room at the break of dawn.

"How's Pepitto?" Becky asked, looking past the proprietress. There was no sign of the little white terrier.

"Oh, he fine, fine," The *signora* replied, beaming. "He back with *mio marito.* The little *generale.* He know he not allowed outside like that."

"Marito?" Becky fumbled over the word.

"Husband," Kate said, grabbing Becky by the arm and pulling her towards the elevator. *"Buona notte, signora."* She waved, forcing a smile.

"Buona notte, signorinas." Another flash of tiny, angled teeth, and the *signora* retreated back behind the desk, reaching for a fresh *sigaretta.*

"Wha…" Becky's mouth worked as the lift clanged shut and began to lurch towards the fifth floor. "Who knew she had a husband?"

"Who knew she had a dog?" Kate grinned a little; the dark cloud that had been draped over her consciousness for the past few hours dissipated.

Back in their room, both women moved about slowly, exhausted after their long day. It was all Becky could do to slip into a sleep-shirt and tumble into bed.

After a few moments, in a room lit only by the pale light from the window, she heard Kate slip into bed. Tired though she was, her breath quickened at the feel of the pilot's long arm draping over her, pulling her close. Even now, Becky reveled in the heat of her, a delicious contrast to the coolness of the fresh sheets.

"Rebecca, did you have a nice day, today?" Kate asked, her voice soft and velvet in the darkness.

"Yes, thanks to you." Becky rolled over slightly so she could trace her hand down the curve of Catherine's side. She gasped when she felt the smooth, warm skin she found there. "Wow."

"Does it bother you?" Blue eyes glittered at her in the moonlight.

"No," Becky chuckled, "not at all. You did warn me, you know."

"You sure? Because I could always throw something on—"

"I absolutely forbid it." Becky placed a warning finger over the pilot's lips. "What makes you comfortable makes me comfortable. In more ways than one," she said, snuggling closer to the welcoming, naked form next to her.

A gentle breeze lifted the window curtains, and there was quiet for a time, save for the sound of two beating hearts. Finally, Becky could hold back no longer. She had to talk about it. For both their sakes.

"Kate," her voice was barely a whisper, "where did you go tonight?"

A long pause, and then, "I'm sorry if I—"

"No… don't be sorry," Becky insisted, "not after giving me this wonderful day. It… it's just that I lost you for a while. And I don't know why."

No response from the pilot. But Rebecca could hear the catch in her breath; feel the tightening of the muscles beneath her skin.

"I know… I talked too much," Becky continued, blushing in the dark at the memory. "Probably too much wine."

"In vino veritas," Kate said, lightly brushing Becky's blonde hair with her lips.

Becky groaned. "More Italian?"

"Nope." Kate released a low rumble of a laugh. "Latin. *In wine, there is truth.*"

"Oh, great. Well, I sure spouted off a lot of truth tonight, didn't I?" She held the heel of her palm to her forehead.

"That's okay, Rebecca," Kate said, and she meant it. "It's just that… this holiday… just the two of us, it won't last forever."

"I wish it could." Becky's voice was suddenly fierce, and her green eyes flashed like gemstones. "I don't want it to end. I *want* it to last forever."

"Easy… sssh." Kate could sense the fear in Rebecca, and tightened the hold she had on her. "I'm not letting you out of my sight. But you know what I mean. We'll go home – and there's a lot of… stuff, we'll have to deal with then. I guess that's what I was thinking about tonight. People we know, people we work with. Hell – I don't even know where your home base is. It's going to be plenty more complicated than just dealing with poor Nathan and Cindy."

"I know," Becky softly replied, understanding the reality of that statement, "I know. But we'll get through it Kate, I know we will. Together."

"Together," the tall pilot whispered hoarsely, kissing Becky lightly on the cheek. "Now get some sleep."

Some moments passed, and Kate could feel Becky relaxing next to her, hear her breathing deepen. And so she was surprised to hear a slurred "L.A." come from the young flight attendant.

Kate pricked up her ears. "Hanson, you say something?"

"L.A.," Becky repeated sleepily. "My home base."

Catherine smiled and held Rebecca near as the blonde drifted off to sleep.

Home.

Kate had never really felt like she'd had one before, not in a long time, anyway. But lying here, with Rebecca Hanson in her arms, she knew there was nowhere else on earth she'd rather be.

Yes, in the heart of the small, slumbering woman by her side, Catherine Phillips had finally found a home.

0800 hours the next morning saw Kate and Rebecca quickly gulping down a cup of coffee, some juice, and a few chewy, fresh-baked rolls, before escaping the solicitous attentions of Signora Canova. They fell outside into the warm, fresh air of yet another bright Italian morning.

"Whoever did a deal with the sun gods, I thank them," Becky said, gazing up at the brilliant, cloudless, azure sky.

The women decided to spend the morning sightseeing by foot, since the Pantheon was a reasonable walk away through Rebecca's favorite shopping district. And so they traveled through the bustling crowds along the Via Condotti, moving onto the larger Via del Corso, finally turning towards the Piazza della Minerva.

First, they investigated the breathtaking church of Santa Maria Sopra Minerva. The colossal gothic church had some beautiful, angelic frescoes by Filippo Lippi, the monk who taught Botticelli. Walking on the cool stone floor, Kate and Becky could only gaze in awe at the wondrous beauty of the monk's handiwork.

Leaving the church, they moved across the sun-dappled *piazza,* past the charming sculpture of Bernini's elephant bearing an obelisk, towards the majestic domed brick building opposite.

The Pantheon.

"Wow," Becky said, her voice a whisper, as they passed through the great bronze entrance doors. Inside, the sphere of the dome soared upward towards the light and air that entered through its apex, an amazing feat of construction for its time.

The height of the dome was identical to that of the walls, lending a harmonious balance, a nearly religious symmetry to the diffusely lit interior. Indeed, people moved about quietly, speaking softly, admiring the marbled mosaic floor, the serene majesty of the architecture, as though they were in a church.

"This was a church, for awhile, during the middle ages," Becky said, scanning the leaflet she'd grabbed at the entrance, "though construction was originally commissioned during the time of Caesar Augustus. 27 BC. Amazing. How did they ever do it?"

"It is impressive," Kate replied, feeling a chill trip through her body in the cooled air. "Tell you what. How about I get a picture of you outside the front doors, where there's light, and we head back so you can get that shopping done?"

"Sounds like a plan," Becky said, tucking the brochure into the backpack Kate carried. She grabbed her camera from the bottom of the bag. "Let's do it."

It took little effort on the young blonde's part to get the attendant at the main entrance to take a photograph of them both. More difficult, however, was the challenge of getting Kate to agree to be in it at all.

"Are you sure?" she hedged, looking away, towards the *piazza.*

"Get over here, you," Becky demanded, pointing to the top step.

Meekly, the tall pilot complied.

Afterwards, working their way back up the Via del Corso, Becky led the way in and out of a dozen shops with practiced ease. She bought Italian leather wallets for her brother and father, a delicate, silk scarf patterned after a formal Victorian garden for her mother, and an exquisitely designed crystal mantel clock for her sister and her husband.

Kate simply stood back in silent amusement as Becky went on her shopping foray, picking things up, admiring them, purchasing them or moving on. Her indulgence of her nieces knew no bounds, as t-shirts, illustrated picture books, and chocolates were added to the parcels the pilot carried.

"Let's drop some this stuff back at the room before we go to lunch, okay?" Kate struggled to get a grip on the latest shopping bag she'd managed to grab from Rebecca.

"Sure," Becky gaily replied, oblivious to Kate's distress. "That'll be more that we can carry this afternoon." Lunch sounded like a good idea to her. Heck, her stomach had growled simply at Kate's mention of the word.

"Let's make sure we get you into a luggage shop," Kate muttered darkly. "I think you're gonna need more with all this stuff."

"*You* have never seen me pack." Becky laughed, heading back through the shopping district towards the Piazza di Spagna.

One of the businesses they passed by was Merona, the boutique where they'd made so many clothing purchases their first full day. "You know," Becky sighed wistfully, "I'd love to go someplace where we could actually wear those nice outfits we each got."

"Really?" Kate's mind skipped back to how stunning the young woman had looked in the coral colored, sleeveless dress she'd modeled.

"Yeah, don't you think it would be fun?"

The pilot considered just how comfortable – or not – she herself might feel in the midnight black sheath Hanson had pressed her to buy. But dammit, she remembered how good the gown had felt on her when she'd tried it on, and Rebecca had seemed to like it well enough. Maybe having a reason for wearing it... for Rebecca... would make it all tolerable.

"Okay."

"What?" Becky's green eyes popped open wide in the sunlight.

"I said 'okay'." Kate grinned down at her surprised companion. "We'll do it tonight. I know a place in the Grand Hotel. It's called *Le Restaurant.* Real fancy-schmanzy."

"Oh, wow, Kate!" Becky grabbed at the taller woman's arms; nearly causing her to drop the carefully balanced packages she carried. "I've heard about that place. Wait until I tell Cindy. It's sooooo chic. And so expensive though, isn't it? Our outfits will fit in perfectly there, don't you think? And can we get a reservation on such short notice?" She paused to take in a heaving breath.

"Terribly. Of course. And just watch me, to answer all your questions," Kate replied, chuckling at Rebecca's exuberance as the Ausonia

came into view. *Just in time,* the pilot considered. Her arms felt as though they were about to
tear off at the sockets. Not that she would ever
mention that fact to Hanson. She still didn't
want her lifting or carrying anything heavy, no
matter how good the young girl proclaimed she
felt.

"Ah... Miss Phillips, Miss Hanson."
Signora Canova's glasses popped off her nose as
she scuttled out from behind the desk towards
them. Anger was written all over her face.

"What is it, *signora?*" Becky reached out a
steadying hand to the older woman's thin, bony
arm.

"He bad man, bad," she cried, wagging a
finger at Kate. "He call back every half hour, all
morning, looking for you. He make me *insano.*
He say he no stop until he talk to you. I say I
don't know where you are." She waved her arm
in frustration towards the street.

"Who?" Kate demanded sharply, not help-
ing to calm the clearly agitated woman.

At that moment, the phone at the front desk
began to ring, in a series of twin staccato bursts.

"Him again," the *signora* swore darkly at
the telephone. "You no have to speak to him,
Miss Phillips, if you no want to." She put her
pince-nez back on her face, meaning business.
"I take care of him," she sniffed.

"Answer the phone." Kate's voice was tired. "I'll talk to whoever it is." She put their bags down on an overstuffed parlor chair.

"Geez, Kate." Becky's eyes were clouded with worry. "Do you think it's a reporter?"

Kate ran her fingers through her dark hair. "Nah," she said, smiling faintly. "I have an idea."

"Miss Phillips," the *signora* said tightly, "Is for you." She held the phone away from her body distastefully. "It's *heeem,*" she whispered, handing Kate the receiver.

A deep breath. "Hello."

"Katie," a voice boomed and crackled across the miles. "How the hell are you?"

"Fine," Kate said, turning her back to where Rebecca and the *signora* had begun to softly converse. "How are you, Cyrus? And how the hell did you track me down?"

"I'll never tell." A deep rumble of a laugh. Kate had to hold the phone away from her ear. "The point is," he finally continued, "when are you getting your sorry ass back here. I need you."

"I'm on vacation Cyrus, remember? You told me to have fun." Her voice was petulant, like a child's. "Well, I am."

"Oh yeah... that's right. I did tell you to take some time off, didn't I? That's gotta be the first time in – what – 2 years for you?"

"Four," Kate corrected, laughing aloud at her mentor's feigned absent-mindedness.

"Sorry Katie," he said. "Can you forgive a senile old director of flight operations?"

"Who are you kidding?" Kate was still chuckling. "Why, you're still smarter than guys twice you age."

"Wha– guys twice my age are dead, Katie."

"I know."

"Why you…" Cyrus growled, knowing he'd been bested. At last, he too broke down, and Catherine could hear the smile in his voice. "You sound good. Real good, Katie."

"Thanks." Kate was sincere. "I am." A brief pause and then, "What's up Cyrus, that you've been pestering our Signora Canova here nearly out of her mind?"

"Oh, that one," Cyrus laughed. "I wish she'd been on my team during Desert Storm. She's one hell of a watchdog, Katie. I couldn't get past her."

"She is a bit… protective," Kate replied, fingering the fresh bandage the *signora* had placed on her elbow just that morning. "So, what's up?"

"I need you back here, Katie," Cyrus began pressing his case in earnest, "and that's no joke. All hell is breaking loose over that hijacking episode…"

"I heard."

"Point is... this thing is ready to blow. Orbis stockholders are up in arms, I've got the Feds crawling up my butthole like sandfleas, our passengers and people are scared... worst of all," he hesitated, "I'm not sure what to do about it."

"What's all this got to do with me, Cyrus? All I do is fly planes." Kate turned her head slightly to see Becky and the *signora* chattering away with one another, smiling. Great.

"You can do a lot more than that, Katie, and you know it. With your skills... your training..."

Kate's stomach fluttered a bit, the way it always did when something threatened to knock her off balance.

"I've known you too long, Cyrus Vandegrift." Kate turned her attention back to the receiver. "Cut the bullshit, you old codger, and spit it out, will ya? This call is costing *you* money and *me* patience."

There was nothing but stunned silence on the phone. And then, "Strategic Safety Operations. A new ad-hoc unit of Orbis Airlines specially formed to predict where and how security breaches might occur – preventing them, or containing them. To maximize passenger and equipment safety, and to form liaisons with like-minded representatives of other airlines, governmental and legal bodies, both domestically and internationally."

"Nice." Kate leaned against the *signora's* desk. "Did you stay up all night writing that? And I still don't know what all this has to do with me."

"Isn't it obvious?" Cyrus shouted so loudly Kate could've sworn he was in the next room. "I want you to run the damn thing."

"No," Kate said quickly, shaking her head. "No way. Flying. That's all I want to do."

"It wouldn't be forever," Cyrus pleaded, "just until we figure out what the hell happened here in New York last week. How those assholes got on board. To prevent that from ever happening again."

"Nope. Forget it."

"Please, Katie. I'll even let you fly now and again if that's what you're worried about; throw you in a rotation to keep you sharp. Remember, this unit is only ad-hoc."

"Ad-hoc," Kate's voice was loaded with sarcasm. "Isn't that what we used to call 'secret' back in the Air Force, Cyrus?"

"You can write your own ticket Katie," he continued, studiously ignoring her objections, "pick your own staff, set your budget, get whatever resources you need... I'll make it happen for you. We've got a problem out there, Katie. And it could get a helluva lot worse before it gets better. People could get hurt."

"I don't know, Cy," Kate said, wavering. "How can I be your best choice for this? Hell, a week ago I was quitting."

"Don't forget, Katie, I know you. I know what you can do. And you can do this. For me. For all those people out there who need your help. And... for yourself."

"Cyrus..."

"There's no one I trust more, Katie, and no one who can do this job better. Will you at least think about it – get back here and talk it through some more?"

"You're making a big mistake, Cyrus," Kate said, bowing her head, knowing that in fact she *would* fly back to New York and talk to the man. Because deep in her heart, she wondered whether he might be right. What if those terrorists didn't act alone... had help? What if they were a part of something bigger, and even more dangerous? What if... the next time, a plane didn't make it safely down?

"Come on, Katie." Cyrus could tell he was getting close. "Fly back here. Tonight. We'll talk."

"Okay," the pilot relented with a sigh, "We'll talk. But I'm not promising you a god-damned thing. And I'm not coming back tonight, either."

"Tonight."

"Tomorrow," Kate said, her voice edged with hardness. "I've got plans. Or you won't see me at all."

"Tomorrow it is, Katie." Cyrus' voice was cheery, now that he'd gotten his way. "See you then." And he cut the connection before Kate had a chance to reconsider.

What the hell just happened here? the tall woman wondered, carefully lowering the receiver back into the cradle. *Damn that Cyrus!* But she had to admit it: the prospect of what he'd proposed sounded intriguing. Well, he had a helluva lot more explaining to do before she would even remotely consider giving him a *yes*.

"Kate, guess what?"

Catherine turned to see Rebecca moving towards her, smiling. God, was this beautiful young woman really hers? "What?" Kate answered, feeling an easy grin spread across her face. Rebecca seemed to have that effect on her, she considered.

"The *signora* has invited us to lunch. With her *husband*," Becky said slowly, rolling her eyes back towards where the *signora* stood expectantly, her hands clasped in front of her. "And *gelato* for dessert. I'd love to go. Wouldn't you?"

Kate could tell that Rebecca was worried that she wasn't up for such an adventurous luncheon. Hell, Hanson didn't know the half of it.

"Sounds wonderful. *Grazie, signora, si.*"

"Uh… great." Becky looked up at her in mild wonder.

Signora Canova beamed. "This way… this way." She hurried off towards the rear of the *pensione,* bidding Kate and Becky to follow her.

"Who was on the phone?" the flight attendant asked. She circled her arm around the pilot's waist as they followed the *signora* towards formerly forbidden territory. "Everything okay?"

"That was Cyrus," Kate said. "Blowing smoke and rattling his saber. I'll tell you about it later. And yes," she added, "everything's okay." She dipped her dark head to softly press her lips against Rebecca's golden hair, stealing a quick lung-full of her sweet welcoming scent as she did so.

Her life. Her love. Her home.

"Everything is *very* okay."

Coming next from
Yellow Rose Books

*Breaking Away**
By Tonya Muir

In <u>With Faltering Steps</u>, with the world of horse racing as a background, Lacey Montgomery meets Rachel Wilson while she is investigating horse trouble for her Mafia boss, Vinnie Russo. While Lacey enlists Rachel's help in getting to the bottom of the horse mystery, the mafia crony learns about life, herself and falling in love. In <u>Making Strides</u> Lacey and Rachel are just settling into their lives together and raising Rachel's daughter, Molly, when Lacey's past strikes back, throwing both women into a whirlwind of crime and fear while they try to overcome a traumatic history and ensure themselves a domestic future.

Available – May 2000.

Available soon from
Yellow Rose Books

Seasons: Book One
By Anne Azel

The first two of four stories about Robbie and Janet over the course of a single year. They deal with elements of Robbie's career in film and Janet's in education. They also examine the crises that can come into the average woman's life. Seasons focuses on the courage that it takes to be female and/or gay in today's society.

Mended Hearts
By Alix Stokes

Two little girls meet at a hospital and become best friends. One of them undergoes open-heart surgery. They are separated, but meet again 24 years later. By now, the older girl, Dr. Alexandra Morgan, is a brilliant Pediatric Heart Surgeon. The younger girl, Bryn O'Neill, is a warm and loving Pediatric Intensive Care nurse. When they meet, they feel an instant connection. Will Dr. Morgan's tortured past keep her from remembering their childhood friendship?

Bar Girls
By Jules Kurre

A very taciturn and brooding English major is brought out of her shell by one very stubborn and talkative young woman she frequently meets at a bar.

Encounters
By Anne Azel

Encounters is a series of five stories: Amazon Encounter, Turkish Encounter, P.N.G. Encounter, Egyptian Encounter, and Peruvian Encounter. The stories are interrelated by the characters who all share a common ancestor. A loop in the space/time continium allows the couples of today to help their ancestors find their own troubled path to happiness.

Other titles to look for in the
coming months from
Yellow Rose Books

Tiopa Ki Lakota By D. Jordan Redhawk
(Summer 2000)

Seasons: Book Two By Anne Azel
(Summer 2000)

Tumbleweed Fever By L. J. Maas
(Fall 2000)

Prairie Fire By L. J. Maas
(Fall 2000)

Dr. Livingston, I Presume By T. Novan
(Winter 2001)

None So Blind By L. J. Maas
(Winter 2001)

Daredevil Hearts By Francine Quesnel
(Winter 2001)